SOMEONE SERIES BOOK 4

Someone to MARRY

ROBERT LEWIS

4 Horsemen
Publications, Inc.

4 Horsemen
Publications, Inc.

4 Horsemen Publications, Inc.
1497 Main St. Suite 169
Dunedin, FL 34698
4horsemenpublications.com
info@4horsemenpublications.com

Cover and Typesetting by Autumn Skye
Edited by Kris Cotter

Library of Congress Control Number: 2023937018

Paperback ISBN-13: 979-8-8232-0176-6
Audiobook ISBN-13: 979-8-8232-0175-9
Ebook ISBN-13: 979-8-8232-0177-3

Someone to
MARRY

Dedication

As **ALWAYS,** **I** dedicate this book to my parents, Robert O. Lewis and Dolores C. Lewis. To my darling diva Bonita, who keeps me focused on writing. To my friends, whose love and support keep me going: Randy, Chris, Rodney, Berto, William, Jeff, Brian, and Kalvin. Of course, this is also dedicated to you, the readers.

Table of Contents

COFFEE AND SEX

THE EARLY MORNING sun stirred Mark awake. Opening his eyes, he saw he was alone in the California king bed. Yawning and stretching, he forced himself to get up to look for the man with whom he shared the bed and, soon, the rest of his life. Hopefully, he had a fresh pot of coffee waiting, or there would be Hell to pay.

Mark found him in his boxers, standing in front of the coffee maker. He took a moment to admire the 6'6" man he loved. Taking in his strong, broad back and hard, firm ass, Mark wondered why it had taken them so long to get here. Then he remembered: they were young and dumb.

Hugging him from behind, Mark said, "Good morning, Hunter."

Turning in his arms, Hunter embraced him. "Good morning." His hands ventured down to cup Mark's bare ass. "You should put some clothes on. Paris will be here in a bit."

Slipping his hands down the back of Hunter's boxers, Mark said, "He doesn't come in for another hour. I want you now."

"I thought you were saving yourself for our wedding night." Hunter laughed.

"Consider this an undress rehearsal." Mark leaned up and kissed him on the lips. "You should be honored. I'm choosing you before coffee in the morning."

Hunter grinned. "I am. Can't you feel it?"

"I'd rather taste it." As Mark slipped down his body, he pulled Hunter's boxers down.

Wrapping his hand around the base of Hunter's thick eight inches. He stroked Hunter, milking out a pearl of pre-cum. Mark kissed the tip, coating his lips with Hunter's excitement. He ran his tongue over the crown, then ran his tongue along the underside to Hunter's balls.

Hunter spread his legs for Mark and leaned back to push his groin out. Mark took full advantage of the offering, taking one of Hunter's large balls into his mouth. He swabbed his tongue over the fleshy orb. Hunter moaned. Mark gave his other ball the same treatment. He felt Hunter's legs tremble.

Mark felt Hunter's hand in his hair. He pulled back to play with the tip again. Opening his lips, Mark swallowed only the fat head of Hunter's dick. Hunter groaned above him. "Damn, I love the way you play with my dick." Hunter gently nudged Mark farther onto his cock. "Suck me, baby."

Mark took him down slowly, letting the taste of Hunter's cock spread across his tongue. When he reached the base, he used his left hand to fondle

Hunter's balls. Mark pulled back before he started to gag. One last swirl of his tongue, and then Mark started working the hard cock feverishly.

"Damn, this is the best way to start a morning." Hunter fisted Mark's hair and pulled him across his length. "We better not have to do special effects when we film in a few days because of your libido."

Mark pulled off Hunter's cock. Stroking the spit-slick rod, he said, "It will be worth it."

"I'll give you worth it." Hunter pushed Mark back. He covered his lover's body with his own. Kissing Mark, he took Mark's arms and pinned them above his head. Breaking the kiss, Hunter ordered, "Stay, boy."

Hunter kissed his way down Mark's smooth muscular body to his hard six inches. He inhaled Mark's cock down to the base. He pushed two fingers under Mark and maneuvered them between Mark's toned, muscled cheeks. He felt Mark's hole quiver at the touch of his fingers petting it.

"Why are you teasing me?" Mark groaned.

Hunter ignored the question, sucking Mark for another few minutes before pulling off. He lifted Mark's legs up and pressed them into his chest. With Mark's hole before him, Hunter lowered his face between the plump cheeks. His strong, thick tongue brushed the sensitive flesh and swirled it around.

"Fuck, eat my ass," Mark moaned. "I hope we're done before Paris gets here."

Hunter licked up Mark's crack, over his balls, and along his shaft. "Guess we better get to the good stuff then." Hunter reached up on the counter and grabbed the small bottle of olive oil. "We really need to start

3

keeping lube stashed around the house if we're going to be this frisky."

"I'll have Paris order some," Mark growled. "Fuck me already."

Hunter drizzled the olive oil from Mark's cock down the crevice of his ass. Setting the bottle aside, he thrust two fingers easily into Mark. "Better add olive oil to the shopping list."

"Can you just fuck me already?" Mark asked through clenched teeth.

Hunter pulled his slicked fingers out of Mark. Using the oil that coated them, he stroked his cock. "Leave it to me to marry a bossy bottom." Putting a hand on either side of Mark's head, he positioned himself so his cock just tickled Mark's entrance. "Maybe I should fuck it out of you."

"If you must. Just hurry up and fuck me already." Mark's eyes rolled back. Hunter had pressed his cock into him, sliding into Mark as easily as a glove. Mark purred, "Oh, baby."

The sound of slick skin slapping mixed with their moans of pleasure. Mark's body tingled from the familiar feel of Hunter's cock in him. Hunter started out slowly, enjoying the feel of Mark's warm insides. He found his rhythm, leaned down, and kissed Mark. Hunter began pounding into him feverously.

Hunter rose back up. Taking Mark's left leg, he twisted the man's so his left leg rested on his right, but left Mark's back on the floor. Hunter put a steadying hand on Mark's hip, the other he slipped around Mark's cock. He began thrusting into his lover, jerking Mark's cock as he did.

"Just so you know, this is just an appetizer for the honeymoon," Hunter grunted. He slipped out for just a moment when Mark twisted around and got on all fours. "The main course is going to last all night."

Mark arched his back when he felt Hunter's hands on his hips. "The dessert I have planned is going to last all day." He reached under himself and took his cock in hand. "Right there, hit it right." Through gritted teeth, he cried out, "I'm cumming!"

Mark's face clenched, then his cock exploded in his hand, spilling his load onto the tile floor. His body jolted with orgasmic tremors. His ass clenched, squeezing Hunter's cock. Hunter's hands tightened on his hips. He felt Hunter's cock swelling in him. Mark reared back into Hunter, meeting each of his furious thrusts.

"Oh, Hell yeah!" Hunter shouted as his cock exploded in Mark. "Fuck! Fuck! Fuck!" Hunter shouted as his cock rapidly fired. He gave Mark a playful smack on the ass. "No more for you." He slipped out of Mark. "We have work to do."

Mark rolled over to lie on his back. With a satisfied grin, he said, "Shut up and cuddle with me." Mark stretched out his arms. "Come on."

"Spoiled bottom." Hunter laughed as he lay on top of Mark. "I guess this is what I signed up for, huh?"

With Hunter resting on his chest, Mark rubbed his back. "Forever and a day."

"Are you guys done yet?" A voice called from another room.

They both began laughing. Mark called back, "He's just doing his required post-sex cuddling! Come on in Paris!"

"I thought we had rules about this." Paris appeared in the doorway. His wavy, jet-black hair fell down around his head. From where they were, the 5'5" young man almost looked tall. His biceps bulged when he crossed his arms across his toned chest. He looked down at them over his black-framed glasses. "I'm not cleaning this up."

"I will," Hunter chuckled. "By the way, we need more olive oil."

PARIS IN THE MORNING

PARIS WENT THROUGH the refrigerator and cabinets, making a list of groceries they'd need this week. Hunter and Mark were washing off their morning coitus. It had been thirty minutes, meaning they were done with round two and were actually showering now. It amazed Paris that the two had such high libidos, considering their line of work.

Sitting down at the kitchen table, Paris reviewed the list. He added a few items he knew they'd need with guests coming. Then he remembered who the guests were and doubled the order. With Billy and Carlos coming, he knew he'd have to do another grocery order midweek. He was about to send it for approval when he added in bold letters: *lube. Lots of lube.*

With that done, Paris pulled up the shared calendar. Daniel was scheduled to come in today for his normal cleaning day while Mark and Hunter were at the gym. Today, Daniel would be making sure all the rooms were clean and set up for their guests. He'd have to see if Daniel could come in more days this week with the number of people coming to stay.

"Lots of lube?" Mark asked, walking into the kitchen. He thought for a moment, then added, "Good idea." Paris cocked an eyebrow at him. He looked at Mark, then at the jar of bills on the counter. Mark pulled a twenty from his wallet and stuffed it in. "Happy now?"

Paris pushed his glasses back up his nose. "Very. How's everything else on the list?"

"You may have to make a second order with Billy and Carlos coming." Mark poured himself a cup of coffee. "When are they coming again?"

Paris scrolled through his phone. "Billy and Carlos are coming Wednesday. Cameron and Jordan are coming Friday. Dennis and Benjamin are driving up Friday, as well. Cody and Brad should be here tomorrow to do the setup for filming." Paris tapped on the envelope he had left on the table. "Speaking of filming, I found this taped to the front gate."

"Another flash drive application from our faceless twink?" Mark asked, sitting down. Taking the envelope, he opened it. "Awe, this time a note." He sat the flash dive on the table and unfolded the note.

Paris saw Mark visibly stiffen after reading it. "What does it say?" He took the note from Mark and read it aloud. "You'll live to regret not using me."

"Check the cameras again." Mark's voice shook when he spoke. "I want to know who dropped this off."

"Dropped what off?" Hunter entered with his hair still wet.

Paris held up the note. "We got another flash drive with a note."

"Daddy Twink again?" Hunter took the note. After reading it, he sternly said, "Check his social media accounts, too. I want to know who this is."

Paris picked up the flash drive. "Does he really think he'll get hired if he doesn't show his face? Every video he leaves us or posts, he hides his face, whether he's jacking off or fucking some guy."

Hunter sat the note on the table and stabbed at it with his finger as he spoke. "I want to know what he means by this."

"He probably means that you'll regret not using him because he's going to be huge." Paris saw the concern on their faces. "What?"

Mark looked at Hunter before explaining. "Remember when we told you Dennis had the stalker, Billy had the murdering ex, and Carlos found himself in a kidnapping-murder situation?"

"All three are coming here," Hunter added.

"Right. Vaguely threatening note." Paris picked up the drive. "I'm going to have to watch all his videos, aren't I?"

Mark smiled. "Consider it a perk."

"You know you like watching Daddy Twink," Hunter teased. Grinning at Paris, Hunter said, "Remember, if we catch you jerking, we get our money back for today."

Paris glowered at Hunter. "You won't. Why does he call himself Daddy Twink? Isn't that a contradiction?"

"He might be a twink that identifies as a daddy?" Mark shrugged. "I don't care. Find out who he is."

9

Paris groaned. "Fine, but you two are going to be late for the gym." Paris stood. "Oh, and don't forget to put your money in the sex jar, Hunter."

"Why do we do this again?" Hunter rolled his eyes. "This is our house, after all."

"Because you won't let me turn the hose on you two," Paris shot back. "Plus, the money goes to charity. Oh, tell your guests that the same rule applies to them."

Hunter looked at his phone. "Is that why you put 'lots of lube' in bold on the list?"

"Here, let me change that." Paris started typing on his phone. "There. Updated."

Mark read his phone. "Fuck ton?"

"You have nothing to worry about." Hunter put a hand on Mark's shoulder. "The boys only play off-camera with their boyfriends."

"Okay, bosses, this has been fun and everything, but you two have someplace to be." Paris made a show of looking at his phone. "If only there was something, like a calendar, your personal assistant keeps updated with your schedule."

Laughing, Mark stood up. "Okay, we get it. Get out so you can enjoy Daddy Twink's porn."

"Thank you, and I'm not going to enjoy it." Paris winked at them. "Much."

DADDY TWINK AND THE
SERVICE BOYS

WITH HUNTER AND Mark off to the gym, Paris decided to take advantage of the solitude to review the flash drive. Sitting down at his desk in the dining room they had converted into his office, Paris waited for his computer to load up. He wasn't sure watching the videos would help him identify the faceless Daddy Twink.

After the first drive showed up, curiosity had gotten the better of him, and he looked up Daddy Twink on Twitter. The account had a couple hundred followers. He watched a few of the snippets Daddy Twink had posted of his fan content to entice new subscribers and followers. The last time he had checked, Daddy Twink had close to five thousand followers.

The videos of the faceless, toned, sculpted body stroking his impressive cock had lured Paris into following the mysterious stud. It was only recently that he started doing collaboration videos. Anyone who expected to see his face in those was disappointed. Daddy Twink had thought of everything to keep his identity a mystery.

Daddy Twink wore a hood that had patches that covered his eyes. Paris knew that he could see through the patches. Hunter and Mark had a similar one. When he was tasked with washing off the evidence of their love for each other, curiosity had gotten the better of Paris, and he had tried on the nylon hood. It wasn't for him.

With his work computer up and running, Paris inserted the drive into one of the ports then waited for the security scan to complete. He checked the time. Daniel wasn't due to arrive for another thirty minutes. That meant if anything popped up while watching these videos, he'd have plenty of time to solve the issue manually.

The scan finished, and the flash drive automatically opened on the screen. There was one video titled "Twink Daddy and the Service Boys" and another saying, "Read Me." Paris debated which one to click first, ultimately deciding on the video first. The "Read Me" file was probably a simple text file with links to Daddy Twink's socials that Paris already followed.

When the video clip loaded, Paris quickly maximized the player, then settled back in his chair. He could already feel the stirring of excitement in his groin. The title "Twink Daddy and the Service Boys" flashed on the black screen before the scene faded to

"For your consideration." Paris grinned. It seemed he'd be the first to see this video.

The black faded away to the scene. Paris instantly recognized the sun-kissed washboard abdominals and the defined Adonis muscles that dipped down into a pair of solid black boxers. The camera panned out to show Daddy Twink with a young, muscular man on each side of him, with their hands behind their backs.

The man on the left side was a stocky, muscular cub of a man with sandy blond hair that fell down around his face that was just shy of needing to be cut to keep it out of his eyes. On the right side was a toned muscular man with short black hair that lay flat on his head. Both men were wearing matching black jocks that bulged with their excitement.

They stayed perfectly still. Daddy Twink put a hand on the back of each of their heads and guided them to him. They took their hands from behind their backs and began running them up and down Daddy Twink's legs and stomach. They grabbed the top of Daddy Twink's boxers and pulled them down his legs.

Paris knew what to expect when the boxers slid down to reveal Daddy Twink's long, thick cock. He'd seen the hard thirteen-inch beast popping out from the trimmed black groin above the bull balls before, but he still had to vocalize his awe. "Damn, that's huge."

Their hands continued to roam over Daddy Twink's hard, defined body. The blond man was stroking his enormous cock while licking Daddy Twink's abs. The brown-haied man was underneath, lapping at his balls. Daddy Twink simply stood there

with his hands running through their hair as they worshiped his body.

The blond moved down. The brown-haired man up. They sandwiched Daddy Twink's cock between their suckling mouths. They moved along Daddy Twink's shaft, back and forth. It began to glisten with their admiration. Pre-cum dribbled out the tip and over his signature mole on his cock head.

Daddy Twink guided them both back to the base of his fuck rod. He held them still while he moved his hips to thrust his cock through their lips. Undoing his pants, Paris licked his lips, wondering how the fleshy club would feel and taste on his lips. He lifted his hips and slipped his pants and briefs down to free his hard cock.

Spitting in his hand, Paris started stroking his hard, seven-inch cock. He was mesmerized by the impossibly large cock gliding through the two young men's mouths. The man looked so tiny, barely taller than Paris himself, but he had a dick that easily was at least a third of his body weight.

Holding the brown-haired man at the base, Daddy Twink moved the blond to the head. The blond engulfed the crown. He was able to take six or so inches before he started gagging. Pulling off to the tip, he worked what he could of the colossal schlong. Then he was pulled off to move back to the base.

The brown-haired man took his place, swallowing a little more of Daddy Twink's mammoth dick. With nearly nine inches in his mouth, he didn't gag. He held the cock down his throat for almost thirty seconds before pulling off and sucking on the head. He

worked Daddy Twink's dick for a few minutes, then was replaced with the blond.

Paris cautiously pumped his cock, not wanting his own personal explosion to happen before seeing more of the video. Since he was introduced to Daddy Twink's videos, they had become the source of many of his personal eruptions. He wasn't sure how he'd act if Mark and Hunter actually hired him.

The camera panned out. Paris saw that Daddy Twink was standing on a crate, wearing his hood. With the push of Daddy Twink's hands, his service boys dropped to all fours. They moved to face each other. Daddy Twink stepped down. He ran a hand down the brown-haired man's back to slip a finger in his ass, then did the same to the blond.

Pulling his fingers from the men, he moved behind the brown-haired man. Situating himself, Daddy Twink rubbed the head of his cock up and down the brown-haired man's crack, then pressed it into him. His cock seemed to slip in easily, but Paris saw the concentration on the brown-haired man's face. Paris was in awe that he could take that much cock.

The Service Boys started kissing while Daddy Twink started sawing into the brown-haired man. He took almost all of Daddy Twink's man meat without even a whimper. The brown-haired man pulled away from the kiss, tossing his head back before putting his head on the blond's shoulder, who began kissing and licking his exposed neck.

Paris felt the stirring of excitement in his balls. He slowed his stroke, only letting go to spit in his hand again. He wanted to last as long as the video, if

he could. Based on the throb of his shaft in his hand, he was losing that battle.

Daddy Twink slowly pulled out of the brown-haired man. Panting, the man fell to the floor and rolled over. His face was a mix of exhaustion and bliss. The blond leaned down to kiss him. Daddy Twink kneeled behind the blond. He pushed his cock in. Like the brown-haired man, the blond took it all without complaint.

Paris could feel the surge building up in his balls. With the wedding planning, he'd been either too busy or tired to put in the effort to look for a casual hookup. Hunter and Mark were his bosses, but they treated him more like an equal, like family. They joked that he was the gay son they didn't want to sleep with. That's why this wedding was so important for Paris.

Daddy Twink pulled from the blond's ass. The Service Boys continued to kiss. Daddy Twink moved around them to kneel down between the brown-haired man's legs. Lifting the brown-haired man's legs up and holding them at the ankle, Daddy Twink sank his cock almost balls deep into the brown-haired man. He pounded the willing Service Boy without mercy.

Daddy Twink pulled out. The blond rolled over onto his back while the brown-haired man got up on his knees. The brown-haired man pulled the top of his jock under his balls, unleashing his hard seven inches. Daddy Twink was between the blond's legs, slamming his cock into him. The brown-haired man straddled the blond's head to thrust his cock into his eager mouth.

Paris checked the timer on the video. It was almost over, to Paris's delight and dismay. He wanted to watch more, but he was on the verge of exploding. He wasn't sure if he could edge himself any longer. He was slowing his stroke and squeezing his balls with his other hand. His cataclysmic ending was fast approaching.

Daddy Twink pulled out of the blond. The brown-haired man stood up, followed by the blond. They both dropped their jocks and kicked them to the side while Daddy Twink lay down on the floor. He held up his dick for the brown-haired man to squat down on. Once he impaled himself on Daddy Twink's spear, the blond pulled him onto his hard eight-inch throbbing cock.

The brown-haired man started riding Daddy Twink while sucking the blond. Daddy Twink fisted his cock. The brown-haired man was fucking Daddy Twink's hand while he fucked himself on Daddy Twink's dick. There was urgency in their movements. The blond started to face fuck the brown-haired man as the brown-haired man was gripping his legs.

After a while, the blond pulled out and started jerking his cock. He exploded onto the brown-haired man's face. After the last of the pulse, the blond dropped down to his knees. Sliding off Daddy Twink's cock, the brown-haired man stood. He jerked his cock until he was coating the blond's face with his spunk.

The brown-haired man kneeled beside the blond. Daddy Twink stood, his huge cock swinging about. He gripped his cock with both hands and began jerking his cock. Back and forth, his hands greased his rod.

His legs began to shake. A geyser of cum blasted out of Daddy Twink's cock, painting the faces of the two men on their knees.

The scene faded out right as Paris allowed himself to release. His balls drew up tight. Before he could grab something to shoot his load into, white cream shot up across his black polo. He jerked in the chair in the aftermath of his orgasm. He milked out the last drops before letting out a satisfying sigh.

Paris leaned back in the chair, exhausted. He let go of his cock. His spunk-covered hand dropped to the side. He looked down at the white splatters across his shirt. He closed his eyes for a moment to enjoy the euphoric feeling. He took several deep, soothing breaths. He'd deal with the cleanup in a minute.

"Shit." Paris bolted out of the chair when he heard the front door close. He tried to keep his pants up as he rushed to the closest bathroom.

He heard Daniel call out, "Hunter? Mark? Paris? Is anyone here?"

"In the bathroom!" Paris yelled out, shutting the bathroom door.

CAR CONVERSATIONS

MARK WAS BROUGHT out of his thoughts by Hunter's hand on his knee. "Are you okay, babe?" he asked, never taking his eyes off the road. "We can skip the gym if you're not feeling it today,"

Putting his hand on Hunter's, he answered, "I'm fine. It was just that note this morning. It has me a little off-kilter. I'm good."

"Are you sure? I can call Caleb and tell him we can't make it." Hunter's voice was soft with concern. "I'm sure he'd understand."

Mark patted Hunter's hand. "He might, but I won't." Mark took a deep breath and let it out slowly. "I was thinking that maybe we should postpone the wedding while we're studio rebranding."

"Hold on." Hunter pulled into a parking spot by the gym. "We've been planning this wedding for six months. Paris has been making sure everything is perfect. The only person more excited about the wedding than me is you." Hunter paused for a second.

"Paris comes a close third. What's going on? Was it that note?"

Mark squeezed Hunter's hand. Looking at his fiancé, he admitted, "It was the note. It brought up all the stuff that happened last year with Dennis, then with Billy, and then with Carlos." Mark shook his head. "I had to start using Mark instead of Trevor because the world knew who we were, and everyone wanted to book Mark instead of Trevor. Then someone outed Caleb as Mask."

"Hey, that wasn't our fault, and Caleb is happy he's off the force," Hunter defended. "Granted, he's not filming anymore, but now that the trial is over, he's gotten quite a few job offers in the private sector."

Mark shook his head. "I know I'm being silly. That note was probably worded poorly, like Paris said."

"Paris is on it. If Daddy Twink meant anything else by it, we'll nip it in the bud before anything bad happens," Hunter reassured him. "All I want you to do from this point on is relax and stay excited about the wedding."

Mark laughed. "Okay, I will." He smiled at Hunter. "If everything turns out okay with Daddy Twink, why don't we hire him? I'd love to see if that dick is as big in person as it looks on video."

"I'll admit I thought about it," Hunter admitted. "It's just that we haven't heard him speak or seen his face. That's a big red flag for me. Plus, we haven't seen him fuck many people. He has a big dick, but we don't know if he knows how to use it."

Mark smirked. "Trust me, he knows how to use it. He's been doing collaborations. I almost subscribed to see the whole video."

"That name, though, Daddy Twink." Hunter sneered when he said the name. "Twinks can't be daddies."

Mark scoffed. "As someone who has made a career by being fucked by twinks, twunks, and twanks, I assure you they can be." Mark winked at Hunter. "They just can't be my daddy."

"Okay, okay." Hunter laughed. "How about instead of thinking about Daddy Twink rearranging your insides, you think of all the hot men we're going to be seeing on our honeymoon?"

Mark closed his eyes and sighed. "I can't believe you booked us a month-long trip touring Europe."

"I knew you've always wanted to go." Hunter leaned over and kissed Mark softly. "The added bonus is no one will know who we are."

Grinning, Mark opened his eyes. "I just hope we keep to our itinerary without Paris there."

"I could always slip him into my pocket," Hunter joked.

Mark covered his mouth to keep from laughing. "That's not funny."

"Yes, it was." Hunter grew serious. "You know, this is going to be the first time our entire family is going to be here, together."

Mark heard the unheard pain in Hunter's voice. "Still no word from Alex?"

"No." Hunter paused. "Wait, you knew I invited him?"

Mark patted the hand on his knee. "Babe, I saw your face when Carlos told us he got hit by a car."

"We filmed so much with him before he moved to the West Coast and we started our studio. He was such a good guy. I don't know what happened." Hunter shook his head. "I know he hurt Dennis, and was an ass to Billy, Jordan, and Cameron. I just hoped he'd, I don't know, come around. I hoped he would respond to the wedding invite."

Mark squeezed his hand. "Hey, you reached out. That's all you can do."

They both jumped at the knock on their window. They looked to see Caleb standing on the driver's side. "Hey, are you guys just going to sit in the car all day, or are we going to work out?"

22

DADDY'S BITCH

PARIS TIMIDLY STEPPED out of the bathroom, hoping he'd gotten all the evidence of his personal enjoyment off his black polo. He cautiously moved down the hall, listening for Daniel. He knew he wasn't caught, but he felt guilty for self-pleasuring himself at work. Stepping back into his makeshift office, he found Daniel sitting at his desk with Daddy Twink's video on the screen.

"Shit," he said under his breath.

Daniel spun in his chair to look at Paris. "Hey, had to release some pressure after watching this video?"

"No," Paris said defensively. "I got something on my shirt, and I had to clean it off."

Daniel chuckled. "Well, that something is still on your shirt."

"What?" Panicked, Paris looked down at his shirt to see little white rings from where he had wiped. His face flushed red with embarrassment. "Oh, God."

Getting up from the chair, Daniel asked, "Is that what you said when you blew your load all over your shirt?"

"Can we, please, not talk about this?" Paris asked, flustered.

Daniel shrugged. "Fine by me. Just one question, though." Paris reluctantly looked up into Daniel's piercing blue eyes. "Are you going to wear your tie-dye sperm shirt all day?"

"Fuck. I need to go home and change. I made a list of things we need done. I won't be long." Paris turned to leave, but Daniel caught him by the arm.

When Daniel spoke, it was a command, not a request. "Wait."

Paris did. He wasn't sure why he did. Daniel wasn't intimidating. He was barely taller than Paris. He was lean with short straight brown hair that he brushed forward and to the side, giving him that innocent boy-next-door look. He was a twink. His deep rich coffee voice, though, was pure daddy.

"Take your shirt off, and I'll throw it in the wash." Again, when Daniel spoke, it was as an instruction, not a suggestion. "There's no point in driving home when there's a perfectly good washer and dryer here."

Paris didn't have a chance to debate the option before Daniel took it upon himself to tug his shirt up. "Hey! What are you doing?!" Paris lifted up his arms to allow his shirt to be pulled off. He quickly adjusted his glasses, then crossed his arms across his chest. "You could have at least let me find a shirt to wear first."

With Paris's shirt in one hand, Daniel used the other to push Paris's hands down off his chest. "Don't do that."

"Do what?" Paris crossed his arms again.

Daniel moved them down again. "That. You're trying to hide yourself. Don't do that."

"I'm not." Paris started to move his arms back up, then stopped. "Okay, I was. I don't like people looking at my body, okay?"

"Makes them jealous or want you, huh?" Daniel winked at him.

Paris glowered at Daniel. "No." He crossed his arms across his chest. "Are you making fun of me?"

"I would never." Daniel reached out and touched Paris on the arm. "You make sure I get paid." When he saw his joke didn't make Paris smile, he added, "I wasn't joking. You have a beautiful, sexy body. I know a lot of guys who would fall over themselves to get to know you."

Paris timidly lowered his hands. "Really?"

"Really." Daniel squeezed his arm. "Let me go put this in the wash, and you can go find a shirt or finish watching your Daddy Twink video."

Paris smiled. "Thanks." Paris was about to leave to find a shirt, but stopped to ask, "How did you know I was watching a Daddy Twink video?"

"You left the video on repeat." Daniel shrugged. "I saw it on the opening credits when it looped."

Paris didn't remember doing that but figured he had since the video was playing when he got back. He headed back into Hunter and Mark's room. He knew their normal clothes wouldn't fit him, but he could

find something he could cover up with. He only had to be creative.

Slipping on one of Mark's crop tops, Paris returned to his office to see Daniel sitting at his desk reading the list of duties he had left. The video was still going. Daddy Twink was having his cock and balls worshiped, so it meant it was the beginning of the video. Paris wondered for a moment what it would be like to be so commanding and confident.

Daniel must have sensed he was there because, without looking up, he said, "This is a lot to get done today. What do you want me to do?" Daniel looked up and tried not to laugh. "What are you wearing?"

"One of Mark's crop tops." Paris lifted his arms up beside him, showing the baggy sleeves and the words, *Daddy's Bitch*, across the chest. Paris felt oddly free wearing something so bold. "Do you like?"

Daniel shook his head. "Are you 'Daddy's Bitch?'" He nodded over to the monitor. "Or are you Daddy Twink's bitch?"

Lowering his arms, Paris walked over. "Neither. I'm nobody's bitch." He leaned over Daniel to turn the video off. "This shirt really isn't me."

"I don't know." Daniel rubbed his smooth chin in thought. "I think you should design your entire wardrobe around 'Daddy Bitch.'"

Paris darted his eyes away from Daniel. "I don't have the attitude for that."

"You totally could." Daniel reached out and adjusted Paris's shirt. "I bet you were mister popular in high school. I'm betting you had all the boys and girls drooling when you wore your short gym shorts."

Paris rolled his eyes. "I went to a private all-boys school."

"Okay, so just the boys." Daniel winked at him.

Paris moved away and leaned against the desk. "No, I went to school with a bunch of networking rich assholes. I mainly stayed in my room, reading my books and comic books."

"I went to public school and hated reading." Leaning back in the chair, Daniel put his hands behind his head. "I was very popular in high school. I barely graduated. I spent all my time partying and driving my parents nuts."

Paris laughed. "Do you know how I drove my parents crazy? I chose to go into entertainment management instead of finance like they wanted. Then I took this job."

"I bet that pissed them off." Daniel leaned forward, resting his elbow on his knees.

Paris crossed his arms, then uncrossed them nervously. "What about you? Did you go to college?"

"I flunked out my freshman year." Daniel shrugged. "My parents kicked me out. It took me a while to get my act together. I've went to school at night and worked odd jobs during the week."

Intrigued, Paris asked, "What did you go to school for?"

"I started out in business, but after doing those odd jobs, I found my passion for cooking. That's why I concentrated in hospitality management. I pushed myself to the limits and graduated earlier this year." Daniel spread his arms wide. "That's why I'm here."

Paris cocked his head, confused. "Wait. What?"

"I'm saving up to go to culinary school." Daniel laughed, lowering his arms. "I clean houses during the day. I work at a catering company. I dance on the bar at Fae Boys and some other stuff."

Wide-eyed, Paris said, "You're a go-go boy?"

"Yeah, you should come see me sometime." Daniel winked at him. "Those men would eat you up."

Paris shook his head. "Maybe after the wedding, and my bosses are on their honeymoon." Paris picked up the list off the desk. "In the meantime, we need to get this done by the end of the week."

"Wait." Daniel snatched the list from Paris's hand. "I have to do all this while you're in here jerking it to Daddy Twink?"

"I was not jerking it to Daddy Twink," Paris defended. "Okay, I was when you got here, but it's work. He left a flash drive with a note that bothered Mark. I'm trying to figure out who he is."

Daniel quirked an eyebrow. "What about it bothered Mark?"

"It said we'd live to regret not hiring him." Paris ran his hand through his hair.

Daniel darted his eyes back and forth. "So?"

"One of their friends was kidnapped last year," Paris answered. "Then another friend was almost killed by his psycho high school boyfriend."

Daniel sat back, shocked. "Wow."

"Then another friend went to go do a film and almost got killed," Paris continued.

Daniel's brows knitted together. "Is it safe to know them?"

"Yes." Paris laughed. "Unless you're a twink." Paris made his eyes go big. "Fuck."

"Now, you're fucking with me." Daniel stood. "Not funny."

"Actually, no." Paris found himself lost in Daniel's eyes. He shifted down the desk to put some distance between them. "Remind me to tell you about it sometime, but right now," Paris snatched the list out of his hand, "you have work to do."

"You know, you're right. 'Daddy's Bitch' doesn't suit you." Danielle grabbed the list back. "Bitch does."

VODKA!

"WE'RE HOME NOW," Hunter told a trembling Mark soothingly as they walked into their home. He had one hand on Mark's back, the other holding his hand. "I'll have Paris make you some tea, and you can lay down for a bit."

Mark's voice shook when he spoke. "No tea. Vodka."

Hunter squeezed his hand. "I don't think—"

Mark shot him an angry look. "I said vodka."

"Okay, vodka. Let me tell Paris we're here, and I'll get you the biggest screwdriver to sip while you lay down." Hunter guided them a few more steps into the house.

Despite his best efforts, Mark couldn't stop shaking. "Hold the orange juice. Straight vodka."

"Okay," Hunter placated. They took a step into the converted office, where Paris was busy at his computer. "Hey, Paris, we need to reschedule that meeting with the caterer."

With annoyance evident in his voice, Paris turned around and asked, "Why?" His tone quickly turned to concern when he saw Mark. "What happened?" Paris stood. "Are you two okay?"

"Yeah, we are." Hunter raised an eyebrow when he saw Paris's shirt. "Are you wearing Mark's crop top?"

Paris looked down at himself and flushed red. "Uh, yeah, um."

"Paris, I got your shirt out of the dryer." Daniel froze when he walked in and saw Hunter and Mark standing there.

Hunter looked at Daniel, then back at Paris. "Do I want to know?"

"You see, um…" Paris began fidgeting nervously.

Moving over to Paris, Daniel handed him his shirt. "He spilled something all over his shirt, and instead of going home to change, I offered to wash it for him."

"I needed something to wear while it was in the wash," Paris explained, embarrassed.

Mark narrowed his eyes at the words on the shirt. "'Daddy's bitch?' Of all my crop tops, you chose that one?"

"I know, he should have looked for one that just said, 'Bitch,'" Daniel joked. He noticed how pale Mark was. "Are you two okay? Mark looks as white as a ghost."

Everyone heard the fear in Mark's voice when he said, "Someone tried to kill us."

"What?!" Daniel and Paris said at the same time.

Hunter squeezed Mark's hand. "A car ran a red light and almost hit us when we were crossing the street. Caleb pulled us out of the way just in time."

31

"Oh, my God." Paris rushed over to Mark's side. "No wonder you're shaking."

Mark leaned into Hunter for comfort. "It was Daddy Twink. I know it."

"We don't know that," Hunter corrected. "Paris, did you find anything?"

Daniel spoke up. "I'll go make Mark some tea."

"Vodka!" Mark called after him.

Paris rolled his eyes. "Why do you think it was Daddy Twink?

"Because of that note," Hunter answered. "Did you find out anything about him?"

Paris shook his head. "I don't think it was him. There was a 'Read Me' file on the drive, too. It was him saying all these studios and guys wanted to make content with him, but he wanted you guys to be who he took the next step with."

"Then what was with that note?" Mark asked.

Daniel yelled from the kitchen, "I can't find the vodka, but I found the tea!"

"It's in the freezer!" Mark yelled back.

Daniel yelled back, "You're getting tea!"

"How about we go shower, and you can sip your tea after?" Hunter suggested. "If you want vodka after, you can have it. Okay, Love Muffin?"

Mark huffed. "Fine, but I want to know who this Daddy Twink is."

"In the video, he was working with two guys called 'The Service Boys.' Maybe I can find something through them," Paris responded. "Oh, and I'll get you your shirt back after I change."

Hunter winked at him. "It sort of suits you. I'll see if they have one in your size." Hunter kissed Mark on the head. "Come on, let's get soapy together."

"You're not going to distract me with sex," Mark grumbled as they started down the hallway.

Hunter pulled him close. "Good, because I'm tapped out for a while. Twice last night and twice this morning. You've got to let a man recharge."

"Those second times were all on you." Mark playfully hip-checked him. "Not that I minded."

Stepping into their bedroom, Hunter pronounced, "Well, you're filming in two days, so no more sex until after the scenes."

"Do you think it was a good idea not to tell Paris that Caleb is looking into Daddy Twink, too?" Mark gave his fiancé a squeeze before reluctantly pulling away.

Hunter pulled off his gym shirt and tossed it on the floor. "I don't want him to think we don't have confidence in his skills." He dropped his shorts, revealing the old-school white biker jock he was wearing. "Caleb still has connections to the force. Remember, before he was Caleb or Mask, he was Detective Briggs."

"I wonder who outed him as Mask. He wore a mask, and you digitally altered his eyes and the tattoo on his ass." Mark pulled off his shirt and tossed it on the pile. He looked at Hunter casually groping himself. He directed Hunter to see what he was doing with his eyes, then said, "I think it would be a good idea if we shower separately."

Realizing what he was doing, Hunter jerked his hand away from his crotch. "I think you're right. Mind if I shower first?"

33

"Go ahead. I'll help Paris find that vodka." Mark laughed. "Make sure you leave me some hot water."

Hunter pointed a finger at Mark. "You leave those two alone. I don't know what we walked in on, but I have a feeling if we were twenty minutes earlier, we'd be taking money out of that sex jar."

"You think?" Mark plopped on the bed. "No. I think he actually spilled something on his shirt. Paris is too shy to do anything like that here."

Hunter shrugged. Right before he stepped into the shower, he said, "I think they'd make a cute couple."

COFFEE TALK

WALKING OUT THE front door, Paris said to Daniel, "Thank you again for staying and cooking. I totally forgot about Cody and Brad with everything going on."

"Not a problem. I told you that I love to cook." Daniel beamed. "Those two don't talk much, do they?"

Paris laughed. "Brad isn't a talker, and Cody is shy around new people. Behind closed doors, though…" Paris shook his head. "There's a reason why they are in the guest house instead of the main house."

"Screamers?" Daniel asked, stopping at his car.

Paris shook his head in thought. "We'll just say that as quiet as they are around people, is how loud they are in private. The last time they were here, Hunter and Mark went to the guest house to sleep."

"Wow. I'd love to see their porn work." Daniel leaned against his car.

Paris nervously ran his hand through his hair. "They don't film anymore. They used to do fan content, but not together. The first time they were together was in the one film they did together last year. It was really hot."

"Hotter than Daddy Twink's?" Daniel teased with a wink.

"No." Paris thought for a moment. "Maybe."

Daniel reached out and adjusted Paris's collar. "Don't let Daddy Twink hear you say that. He may not keep you as a fan."

"Ugh, I messaged him on all his social media, and he still hasn't answered me." Paris groaned. "I did it under my personal account. Do you think I should have done it under the studio's account?"

Daniel brushed his hands down Paris's arms. "It might have helped. He probably gets a lot of fan messages that he just ignores."

"Another strike against him." Paris turned and leaned against Daniel's car with him. "If a performer has his messages on, he should do his best to reply within forty-eight hours. Well, the non-creepy messages."

Daniel nodded. "I did not know that. Good to know."

"Something I learned from Hunter. That's why most have their messages off." Paris pushed himself off the car. "Anyway, I should let you go. I'm sure you have something better to do than talk out here with me."

Daniel flashed him a warm smile. "No. I don't." He pushed off the car. "I like talking to you."

"Oh." Paris felt his cheeks flush red. First, from the thought of Daniel flirting with him, then

embarrassment when he reasoned Daniel was just being friendly. "I like talking to you, too."

Daniel motioned with his eyes back to the house. "How about we go grab a coffee where we're away from snooping eyes?"

"What do you—" Paris turned to the house to see Hunter and Mark duck behind the curtains. "What's with them?"

Daniel plucked Paris's shirt. "They came home, and you were wearing a different shirt because you got something all over it."

"You don't think that they think—" Paris looked to the house, then at Daniel, then back at the house. "Oh, my God, they do, don't they? I need to set them straight. I mean, come on, me and you? That's funny. Like that would ever happen."

Daniel rocked his head slightly in thought. "I don't know. I think you'd settle for a sexy, hard-working guy with a dream, like myself."

"Please, I'd kill for a guy like you." Paris laughed. "Guys like you aren't into guys like me."

Daniel raised an eyebrow. "What do you mean? Guys like me and guys like you?

"Nothing." Paris shrugged.

Daniel narrowed his eyes at Paris. "Uh-huh. We're coming back to that."

"I should go. I need to find a way to make sure there's food for everyone in the morning." Paris started to turn to walk away.

Daniel stopped him by taking his hand. "Do you cook?"

37

Paris glanced down at Daniel's hand holding his before nervously looking up. "No. Hunter does, but he has a full schedule tomorrow."

"My boss already said it was okay for me to come every day this week to keep the house up; why don't I help you out with the cooking?" Daniel asked, running his thumb over the top of Paris's hand.

Paris sucked on his lower lip, then his face brightened with a smile. "Okay, only because you'll already be here. We have to pay you, though."

"Look at me, making you smile and solving all your problems so you can go have coffee with me." Daniel winked at him. "I'm your twink daddy."

Paris couldn't help but laugh. "It's Daddy Twink, and twinks can't be daddies."

"Meet me at Grind House and I'll tell you how you're wrong about that." Paris tried to pull away, but Daniel wouldn't let go. "I mean it. I want to hang out with you."

Paris sucked on his teeth as he pretended to debate it. "Fine. I'll meet you there." Paris tried to pull away, but Daniel kept hold of his hand. "I promise." Paris laughed. "I'll be there. You can let go."

"You better. I'm going to have a drink waiting for you." Daniel let go of his hand. "What do you want?"

Paris crossed his arms. "Oh, I get to make a decision?" he playfully said. "An oat milk hazelnut mocha latte."

"Got it." Daniel opened his car door. He motioned back to the house with his head. "Go ahead and yell at the super-sized gays. I'll be waiting."

Paris stepped back and let Daniel get into his car. He watched the young man pull away, then turned back to the house to see Mark and Hunter dive behind the curtains again. He started toward the house, only to stop and turn around. He smiled impishly. *Let them wonder. That'll teach them to be nosey.*

Pulling into an empty parking spot, Paris wasn't sure why he was nervous. It was coffee with Daniel. It wasn't a date. They were just two friends having coffee. Granted, in the four months since Daniel started cleaning for them, they didn't talk about anything except business before today.

Stepping into Grind House, he saw Daniel at the counter, talking to the barista. The barista tipped his hat toward Paris. Daniel turned around, holding two cups of coffee. That was when Paris noticed Daniel had changed out of his baggy tee into a form-fitting tank top that showed off his sleek, toned body.

Paris stood there, gawking. He wasn't aware that Daniel was hiding a tight, toned body with hard, sculpted muscles under those baggy clothes. Paris's eyes drifted down Daniel to see his body tapered to a perfect V before billowing out with his baggy jeans.

"Are you okay?" Daniel asked, moving over to one of the tables and setting their coffees down. "Come on, before your coffee gets cold."

Paris swallowed hard, then managed to get out, "You changed." He forced his feet to move to the table. "I didn't realize you were so, um, fit."

"Yeah, I'm a go-go boy, remember?" Daniel put his hands up over his head, pulling up the bottom of his tank top and revealing the bottom of his slender

waist that he swayed back and forth. "Do you like my moves?"

Paris wetted his lips. "Uh, yeah."

"Too bad those are his only moves," the barista called from behind the bar. "Luckily, he has a big—"

"Personality." Daniel cut him off. He shot the barista a dirty look before sitting down. "Sit. Let's talk."

Paris sat down, still a little flustered by Daniel's sexiness. He wrapped his hands around his coffee and turned it around and around before finally asking, "How do you know the barista?"

"He dances on the bar, too." Daniel called over his shoulder, "Just not as good as I do!"

The barista called back, "Fuck you!"

"I'm a top!" Daniel yelled back before returning his attention back to Paris. "You should come see us. You'll have fun. I promise."

Paris took a sip of his drink to keep from answering. Warm hazelnut flavor washed over his taste buds. When he saw Daniel was waiting for a response, he said, "I'm not really a bar person."

"That's cool." Daniel took a sip of his coffee. "What do you like to do in your free time? Tell me about Paris." He leaned back in his chair. "What is Paris like when he's not babysitting adult film stars?"

Paris quickly glanced at the barista. There was something familiar about him. He returned his attention to Daniel. "I read. Mainly science fiction, superhero stuff. I really don't do much else. Books were my escape in school and are sort of my escape now."

"I'm not much of a reader unless it's cookbooks." Daniel laughed. "Maybe you could read to me sometime."

Paris smiled slightly at the thought. "Okay. What do you like to do when you're not cleaning or wiggling your hips on top of a bar?"

"What would I like to do, or what do I actually do?" Daniel leaned forward and took a healthy drink of his coffee. "If I'm not working, I'm in the gym. I hustle man. I messed up my education the first time. I'm not doing it again."

"Couldn't you get loans or help from your parents?" Paris regretted the question once he saw the look on Daniel's face.

Daniel picked up his coffee. Paris wasn't sure if Daniel was going to drink it or throw it at him until he brought it to his lips. Setting the cup down, Daniel said, "My credit is shit, and my parents cut me off financially after I fucked up school the first time. This time it's all on me. That's how it is and how I'm going to do it. On my own terms."

"I understand that." Paris looked down into his cup. "My parents keep pressuring me to find something else, but wearing a suit every day, filling out reports, and making small talk in the break room," Paris shuddered, "that would be a living nightmare for me."

Daniel winked at him. "I bet you look hot in a suit."

"I guess." Paris glanced over at the barista. He had a nagging feeling that he'd seen the man before. "Anyway, I cut myself off from them financially. Of course, I have a trust fund I fell back on."

Daniel downed the last of his coffee. "I wish I had a trust fund to fall back on, but I would have probably burned through it partying if I had it."

"You know if you need money, I could help you out," Paris offered.

Daniel's face immediately hardened. "I'm not a charity case. I can do it on my own."

"I didn't mean to offend you," Paris tried to apologize. "I just wanted to offer some help."

Daniel looked hard at Paris. "I don't need help."

"Relax, man," the barista said, putting a hand on Daniel's shoulder. "You're scaring your date, and you haven't even dropped your pants yet."

Daniel looked up at the barista, then back at Paris. His face softened. "Sorry. In my experience, nobody offers you money unless they want something from you."

"I only wanted to help out a friend who helped me out today." Paris pushed his glasses up the bridge of his nose.

Daniel looked up at the barista. "We're good, Terry."

"If you really want to help this guy out, convince him to have a little fun. He's all business." Terry gave Daniel's shoulder a squeeze, then walked off.

"He's always getting on me to cut loose," Daniel groaned. "He doesn't get it."

Paris surprised himself when he reached out and took Daniel's hand. "I get it. You're driven, but you need to have fun, too." Paris rolled his eyes at the irony. "Which is what Hunter and Mark keep telling me."

"Workaholic, too?" Daniel asked, rubbing his thumb over Paris's hand. "We're a pair, aren't we?"

Paris looked down at their joined hands. "Maybe we could, I don't know, help each other have fun?"

"I'd like that." Daniel gave his hand a squeeze.

Paris shyly looked up at Daniel. "Maybe you could take me to see you dance?"

"I'd like that." Daniel grinned at him. "Maybe you could read to me?"

Paris smiled back at him. "I'd like that."

SOMEONE'S IN THE KITCHEN

MARK **WOKE UP** cradling Hunter. His hard cock escaped the jock he wore to bed and was pressed against Hunter's firm, muscled ass. It never failed. When they went to bed, Hunter was always the big spoon, but when they woke up, Mark was the big spoon. He liked it, holding his big strong man and protecting him while he slept.

Mark ran his hand up and down Hunter's chest, feeling the slight heave of his chest as he slept. He was tempted to venture lower and take hold of the hard cock he knew waited for him, but he controlled himself. He knew that if they started, they wouldn't stop. It would be fun at the moment, but Hunter would chastise him after. Mark was filming soon.

Carefully, Mark unwrapped himself from his love and slipped out of bed. He tucked his cock back into his jock and slipped into his sleep pants before heading to the kitchen. If he couldn't treat his man with morning sex, he could at least make sure he woke up to fresh coffee, maybe even make him some toast.

In the hall, he paused when he heard someone moving about in the kitchen. Fear gripped Mark. It was too early for Paris. Brad and Cody had their own stocked kitchenette. With his heart beating a mile a minute, he cautiously moved forward until he was at the door. He peered around the corner.

"Mother fucker!" Mark exclaimed when he saw Daniel working in the kitchen. "What are you doing here?"

Daniel froze, his eyes darting left, then right, before landing on Mark. "Making breakfast for everyone."

"That's not what I meant," Mark said, coming around the corner. "You scared the shit out of me."

Daniel grabbed a pair of pot holders and opened the oven. "I guess Paris didn't tell you he hired me to do the cooking this week?" Daniel pulled out a pan of fresh croissants. "There's fresh coffee. Do you want me to make you some eggs?"

"No, he didn't." Mark poured himself a cup of coffee. He took a moment to enjoy the smell of Daniel's work. "Do I smell bacon?"

Daniel opened the microwave above the stove, revealing a plate covered with a paper towel. "Bacon and sausage." He pulled the plate out. Uncovering the meat, he held it out to Mark. "Want some?"

"I'll wait for everyone else," Mark answered, resisting temptation again. He watched Daniel recover the plate and put it back in the microwave, then he started brushing melted butter over the croissants.

Since they were alone, Mark decided to be blunt. "What are your intentions with Paris?"

Daniel stopped what he was doing and turned around. "My intentions? You sound like a father from the 1950s whose virginal daughter is being picked up for a date by the town bad boy."

"I'm not that old. Paris is far from virginal." Marked sipped his coffee. "You, you might be the town bad boy."

Daniel grabbed a dish towel to wipe his hands. "I was, but not anymore. Paris is a cool guy. We're friends. Nothing more." Daniel slung the dish towel over his shoulder. "I don't have time for romantic or sexual interests right now. I'm saving up for culinary school."

"Is that so?" Mark folded his arms across his bare chest and leaned against the counter. "You don't have any nefarious plans at all?"

Daniel laughed. "You're using some big words for someone barely into his first cup of coffee."

"I was scared awake by hearing a person I wasn't expecting in my kitchen," Mark shot back.

Daniel mirrored Mark's stance. "Touché. Well, to answer your question, I don't have any nefarious plans for Paris. He needs someone he can just be himself and have fun with, but stay focused. I do, too." Daniel shrugged. "I think we're good for each other."

"Daniel? What are you doing here?" A groggy Hunter asked from the doorway, wearing a pair of sleep pants and an old tee that had more holes in it than Swiss cheese. He ran a hand through his bed-ridden hair. "Is there coffee?"

Mark turned and poured his fiancé a cup of coffee. "Paris hired him to cook for us." Mark added a spoon of sugar to Hunter's morning elixir. "They're friends now."

"Good," Hunter said, slipping his arms around Mark and kissing him on the cheek. "We're going to be busy with the wedding and filming." Hunter took the coffee from Mark and slipped away. "Paris and Daniel are friends. What do we think about that?" Hunter asked before sipping his coffee.

"We don't know yet," Mark answered, turning to eye Daniel. "I think you need to threaten his life."

Hunter looked at Mark questioningly. "Why would I threaten Paris?"

"Not Paris, Daniel." Mark shook his head. "Go drink your coffee."

Daniel covered his mouth to hide his amusement. "You two are hilarious. I hope I find what you two have one day."

"It's easy. Get into porn," Hunter joked. He gave Mark a kiss on the cheek. "I'm going to check my email. Call me for breakfast."

Daniel took a croissant and napkin, then handed them to Hunter. "Just tell me how you want your eggs."

"Sunny side up." Hunter took a bite of the croissant. "Oh my God, that's good. Do we know if Brad and Cody are up yet?"

Daniel's face went serious. "Yes, and I need a hazmat suit to clean that house after what I heard."

"They are loud." Mark grinned. "They'll clean up after themselves and repair whatever damage they

47

do. We need to get the other rooms ready for Billy and Carlos."

"Keep Carlos out of the refrigerator and Billy out of the kitchen," Hunter ordered. "Carlos will eat us out of house and home, and Billy will cook it all up for him."

Daniel nodded. "Got it. Defend the kitchen at all costs."

"I'll go find out how the boys want their eggs. I want mine scrambled." Mark pointed a finger at Daniel. "Don't think this conversation is over. Once we're caffeinated, we're revisiting it."

"Understood." Daniel opened the microwave. "Just remember that I made bacon."

Hunter finished the last of his croissant. "There's bacon? Oh, he's got my approval."

"Thank you. Now, why exactly do I need your approval to be his friend?" Daniel asked, pulling two strips of bacon from the plate and handing them to Hunter. "He's not your kid. Is he?"

Hunter took a bite of bacon. "No. He's our adopted gaybe."

"We tend to adopt a lot of children," Mark added.

Hunter finished his bacon. "Stick around long enough, and you'll be adopted in, too."

"Why does that scare me more than it should?" Daniel joked.

Mark shrugged. "Because of everything our little family has been through over the past year? That reminds me, do you know if Paris found out anything about Daddy Twink yet?"

"Nope.," Paris answered, walking in. "He did answer my message and said he was just looking to get signed on. What do you think, Hunter? Think you might sign him?"

Hunter looked at Mark before answering. "No. I don't think he's a good fit for us right now."

"Enough talk. I'll grab the boys. Daniel, scramble those eggs," Mark ordered gruffly before stepping out the door.

TAKE A BREAK

PARIS LEANED BACK in his chair. Closing his eyes, he took his glasses off and rubbed the bridge of his nose. His eyes needed a rest from the screen. The project Hunter and Mark left him to review was interesting. The problem was there was so much to read, and he couldn't stop once he started.

Paris sat his glasses on his desk. With everyone off doing things, he decided to take advantage of the relative quietness of the house. He took a deep breath and let it out slowly, trying to quiet the racing thoughts in his head. There was so much to get done. He just had to get organized.

"Are you okay?" He heard Daniel ask right before he felt Daniel's strong hands on his shoulders start massaging. "Man, you're tense."

"That feels great, thank you," Paris said with a relaxing exhale. "I'm fine. I just have a lot on my plate."

Daniel started rubbing along Paris's neck. "Well, cooking and cleaning is me. Hunter and the loud boys out back have the filming covered. What do you have left?"

"The wedding," Paris groaned. "And now I have this new project Lexi Luscious sent over to Hunter that he wants my feedback on."

Daniel's hands moved into Paris's hair to massage his scalp. "The wedding is next week. When does Hunter want your feedback?"

"Your hands are magic." The storm of thoughts in Paris's head calmed. "He wants me to send it to him on his honeymoon."

Daniel ran his thumbs in circles on Paris's temples. "Then focus on the wedding. Take a day off, then work on the project Lexi Luscious sent."

"Mm, her name is Lexi Luscious, not Luscious Lexi." Paris felt the stress leaving his body. "I would, but it's such a great project."

Daniel patted Paris's chest. "Alright, tell me about it."

"She wants to start her own media production company with its own app that people can stream content on," Paris said, opening his eyes. He picked up his glasses and put them back on. "She didn't expect the video Jordan wrote with Billy in it to become a popular series. A few adult film actors have approached her with their own content ideas since then. She'd love to make them, but it costs money."

Daniel strummed his fingers on Paris's chest. "Create a streaming service, charge a fee, and go from there. Brilliant."

"Right. She figures that if the actors get a quarter of their fans to subscribe, it'll be turning a profit

within two years or less." Paris tilted his head to look up at Daniel. "It's actually more than just a streaming service. There's going to be like a one-stop media hub with articles, stories, and podcasts."

Smiling down at Paris, Daniel said, "Wow, that does sound ambitious. It sounds like a good idea, too. Does she know what she wants on there yet?"

"There's a podcast she wants to put on that she said Cameron was reviewing, and Jordan is working on something hush-hush." Paris looked back at the screen that tormented him. "She figures she needs at least twenty shows before she can launch, but she needs ideas. Good ideas."

Daniel rested his head on top of Paris's. "And you're trying to come up with ideas."

"No, she has proposals from people about what they want to do. I'm going through them and making notes on them. What to change, whether she should make it or not." Paris reached up and patted Daniel's hand. "She wants Hunter and Dennis to go in with her. Dennis has the writing skills, and Hunter has the talent and production skills. They'll work the East Coast while Cameron and Jordan handle the West."

Daniel pulled away from Paris. "What about the adult-oriented stuff?"

"Hunter doesn't want to get out of the industry, but this is an opportunity." Paris found himself missing Daniel's touch. "They could do both, but they would have to put someone they trust in charge of the adult factor."

Putting his hands back on Paris's shoulders, Daniel thought for a moment. "Why not you?"

"I don't have the skills. Besides, I want to manage people, not a company," Paris answered, taking secret delight in Daniel's touch. "I wouldn't know what to do."

Daniel gave his shoulders a squeeze. "Then learn." He patted Paris's chest. "Come, take a break and keep me company. I need to start marinating the chicken for dinner."

Exasperated, Paris said, "I don't have time. There's so much to do."

"You need a break." Daniel's tone changed. Paris couldn't quite place it at first. He knew it, though, and it seemed as odd as it was appropriate. It was a "daddy" voice. "Come on."

Paris stood up and followed. "Fine. Are you always this demanding?"

"When it comes to you taking care of yourself? Yes." Daniel said over his shoulder.

Paris watched Daniel pull out two bags of defrosted chicken. "That's a lot of chicken." Paris. "What are you making?"

"Fried chicken," Daniel answered, dumping the chicken into two large casserole dishes. "Hunter said Billy was from the South, so I figured he might enjoy my take on it." Daniel grabbed a jug of white wine and began pouring it over the chicken. "Plus, Mark asked for it."

Paris watched Daniel move the chicken around, making sure every piece was soaking in the wine. "What else are you making?"

"I was thinking of some honey cornbread, sweet coleslaw, roasted potatoes, and mojito mocktails."

Daniel turned and winked at Paris. "For dessert, I ordered chocolate chip ice cream cookies."

Paris felt a slight flush in his cheeks. "Wow. Cooking to impress. Where did you learn to do all that?"

"Internet." Daniel returned his attention to the chicken. He wrapped the dishes in plastic wrap. "I knew how to cook your basics before, you know, anything out of a box. I once tried to impress an asshole I'd like to forget by making him something out of a box. He took one look at it and laughed at me."

Paris knew he shouldn't ask, but he did anyway. "An asshole? Was he an ex?"

"No," Daniel answered gruffly. "He was someone I thought I wanted to date, but he turned out to be an—"

"Asshole." Paris finished.

Daniel smiled at him. "Tell me about this project. Any good show ideas?"

Paris shook his head. "There are quite a few bad ideas." Paris thought for a moment. "There's a home repair show idea. A round table talk show thing that sounds interesting called 'Bottoms' Brunch.' A few sitcoms I think people might like, a couple of edgy movie ideas, and Jordan's stuff." Paris shook his head.

"What?!" Daniel turned around in mock anger. "No cooking show?!"

Paris contemplated the idea. "I don't remember one. Those are popular. Maybe you could do a cooking show."

"No one trusts a skinny twink to teach them to cook." Daniel turned and grabbed one of the dishes. "Open the refrigerator for me?"

Paris did. "Why not?"

"Never get cooking advice from a skinny chef or sex advice from a nun," Daniel answered, sliding the dish onto one of the shelves. He turned to look at Paris. "Maybe you should run the network and leave the adult films to Hunter and Dennis."

Paris was about to argue against that when he stopped to think about it. "You know. That makes sense." He watched Daniel put the other dish in the refrigerator. "When Hunter gets back, I'll suggest it. Thank you."

"Look at me solving more of your problems." Daniel winked at him. "Does this make me your daddy?"

Paris groaned. "Twinks can't be daddies."

"Yet, I keep proving that wrong." Daniel winked at him before returning to the counter. "You want to watch me bake? I'm a master baker."

Paris rolled his eyes. "I'm going back to work."

WE NEED A NEW CATERER

MARK DIDN'T HEAR any of the hustle and bustle going on around him in the busy coffee house. Sitting at one of the tables, he focused on his breathing while he waited for Hunter to return with their order. He knew that it had something to do with Daddy Twink being mad at them because Hunter hadn't hired him.

"Here, drink up." Hunter sat an iced coffee in front of Mark before taking the seat across from him. He looked into Mark's vacant eyes. He reached out and took Mark's hand. "Are you okay?"

Mark blinked himself back into reality. "No," he answered honestly. "We almost got killed yesterday, and now the caterer is dead."

"Mark," Hunter squeezed his hand, "Caleb tracked down the car from yesterday. It was some punk kid that was late for class."

Mark pulled his hand away, angry Hunter was dismissing his fears. "How do we know he's not lying? That he's not working for Daddy Twink?"

"Caleb questioned him." Hunter smirked. "Thoroughly."

Mark sipped iced coffee. "He's not innocent just because he let Caleb fuck him. He could still be lying."

"Trust me, he wasn't. He's Caleb's plus one." Hunter laughed. "That reminds me, the kid's a vegan, so we need to tell the caterer we need another vegan option." He caught Mark's glare. "Oh, yeah. Sorry, I forgot."

Mark shook his head in disbelief. "Why aren't you taking this seriously?"

"Mark, I know you're freaked out, but we don't know how the caterer died. It was probably an accident or natural causes," Hunter reasoned. "Paris will find us a new caterer." He reached out and took Mark's hand. "No one is trying to kill us. I promise you. If it'll make you feel better, I'll hire Caleb to do security."

Mark gave him a weak smile. "Tell him not to fuck any more of the suspects."

"I can't guarantee that." Hunter patted Mark's hand. "You know that no man is immune to Caleb's charms."

Mark relaxed and allowed himself a laugh. "Lock up your sons and husbands."

"Or share them." Hunter let go of Mark's hand. "Too bad he's not filming anymore. We could put that overactive libido to good use."

Mark watched Hunter take a drink of his coffee. "You want to hire Daddy Twink, don't you?"

"I do, and I don't." Hunter took another drink. "I really wish we heard him talk or saw his face. Having a big dick isn't everything in making movies. You have to know how to use it and be able to perform for the camera."

Mark turned his cup in his hand before taking a drink. "I know he's up to no good. We should agree to meet with him, then spring our trap."

"As crazy as it sounds, maybe we should meet with him." Hunter pulled his phone out. "Then maybe you'll be able to focus on the wedding." He began typing on his phone. "I'm going to tell Paris to set up the meeting. On our terms."

Mark leaned back in his chair. "I bet he won't meet with us. Oh, don't forget to tell Paris that we need a new caterer." Mark took his iced coffee and downed most of it. "Or did you forget about that again?"

"I didn't. I also didn't forget that Billy and Carlos are flying in today." Hunter sat his phone down. "Done. I sent instructions to set up a meeting with Daddy Twink and to find a new caterer. Now, do you want to go home or go to the gym?"

Mark down the last of his coffee. "Gym. I need to work off some of this agitation since I'm saving myself for marriage."

"You're the one that wanted to shoot this week because we'd have the old gang in town and it would help keep your mind off the wedding," Hunter countered. "That one is all on you."

Mark rolled his eyes. "At least we rented a nice house to film in. What did Dennis say the name of the script was?"

"*Office Hours with the Professor*. It's a three-way," Hunter said with a smile. "After two one-on-ones."

Standing up and stretching, Mark asked, "Is Dennis ever going to get back into filming, or is he permanently behind the scenes now?"

"I am permanently behind the scenes. Dennis is thinking about making a comeback," Hunter answered, standing as well. "We talked yesterday. He's happy behind the scenes and working with Jordan on content, but he misses filming. He also mentioned he and Benjamin might move back to the city."

Mark grabbed Hunter's arm to keep him from walking away. "Wait, they're moving into the city?"

"They're thinking about it." Hunter shrugged. "Benjamin has been getting a lot of work requests from here in the city that he keeps having to turn down."

Mark started walking with Hunter out of the coffeehouse. "What are they going to do with the house?"

"The county offered to buy the entire property. They wouldn't be considering it otherwise." Hunter held the door open for Mark. "They want to attract some manufacturing plants or something."

Mark slipped his arm around Hunter's. "Are you really going to completely step away from the adult film industry? This project of Lexi's may not pan out. What then?"

"I was thinking Paris could take over. He's not a director, but we could hire those. That way, we can slide back in if need be," Hunter reasoned.

Mark stopped them both. "Why doesn't Paris do the Lexi project, and you stay in the adult films? It's what you know."

"Lexi wants me," Hunter answered simply.

Mark snorted. "She can want in one hand, shit in the other, and see which one fills up first."

"What?" Hunter asked, torn at whether to be shocked or laugh. "I think you've been talking to Billy too much."

Mark started them walking again. "Maybe, but it still stands. You need to do what's good for you. You have the connections and reputation in the industry, not Paris. Plus, he's basically a prude."

"He is not. Didn't you see that 'Daddy's Bitch' crop top he was wearing yesterday?" Hunter threw his head back in laughter. "It looked like a regular shirt on him."

Mark chuckled. "It did, and you know what I mean. You're in the middle of rebranding. You can't just pass that on to someone else midstream."

"You're right. I'll talk to Paris about it when we get back from our honeymoon. I told him not to look at any of the stuff Lexi sent us until after the wedding." Hunter stopped and looked around. "Did we pass my truck?"

Mark looked about. "No. I don't remember you parking this far away, either."

"Shit." Hunter pulled out his FOB and began clicking the unlock button. He didn't hear a chirp. "Fuck, did someone steal my baby?"

Mark pulled out his phone. "You call the police. I'll call Paris."

60

PORN FANTASY

"**N**OW LAY DOWN and close your eyes," Daniel ordered Paris. "You've been staring at screens all day. You have a headache, and your eyes hurt."

Paris reluctantly climbed onto the bed. "I need to call Hunter and find out why we need a new caterer."

"It can wait. No shoes on the bed." Daniel took Paris's shoes off. "You weren't at your computer ten minutes before you were closing your eyes and rubbing your temples."

Paris settled into the bed. "I was just resting my eyes. Can I, please, have my phone back?"

"No." Daniel draped a blanket over Paris and began tucking him in. "I'll come get you in thirty minutes. Now close your eyes and dream of Daddy Twink."

Paris closed his eyes. "I don't like Daddy Twink. He's not my type."

"Liar." Daniel turned off the lights. "Thirty minutes," he said before shutting the door behind him.

Paris grumbled, "Asshole."

"I heard that!" Daniel yelled through the door.

Paris took deep soothing breaths, trying to quiet the riot of thoughts in his head. One thought kept surfacing. Daddy Twink. Daddy Twink finally responded to his message. Daddy Twink also gave him a free one-year subscription to his fan site that Paris was going to take full advantage of.

Paris went through the myriad of jerking videos and the new videos he filmed with others. Most were with the Service Boys, either together or one on one. There were a few with other guys. They were young, taller, muscular guys, like The Service Boys. It seemed that Daddy Twink had a type.

Paris noticed that all the videos started the same. "Were you a good boy? If yes, you can watch this video," flashed on the screen, then the actual scene title and scene. The video would then play, whether it be Daddy Twink stroking his amazingly huge cock or him sliding into one of his eager and willing bottom boys. At the end of the video flashed, "Did that get you off? Good boy."

Paris thought about the videos. The videos weren't about Daddy Twink. He got off on getting others off. He never kissed, sucked, or ate ass, but he made sure his partners were enjoying themselves. Even in his stroke videos, it seemed like his only goal was to get the viewer off.

If I was with him, Paris thought, relaxing his body, *I'd make it about him.* The fantasy began to evolve in his head as a haze of sleep drifted its way into Paris's mind. *It would be a total porn fantasy.*

An image formed in Paris's mind. Daddy Twink was lying on a raised table, his arms restrained above him. His ankles were tied, so his legs were slightly open. Aside from a towel that covered his pelvis and his mask, he was completely naked and on display for Paris to take full advantage of.

Daddy Twink would be nervous but willing. Relinquishing his power and allowing himself to be restrained was the ultimate sign of trust. A trust Paris would have earned. Putting himself on display was a gift for Paris. A gift he would thoroughly appreciate and enjoy, at least in his fantasy.

Paris would step into view, naked as the day he came into the world. His seven-inch cock would jut out from his perfectly trimmed pubes. With a hand lightly touching Daddy Twink, Paris would move from his left foot to his head. Paris would feel Daddy Twink tense and then relax under the butterfly touch of his fingertips.

Leaning down, Paris would kiss where Daddy Twink's would-be mouth on the mask. Then, with lustful eyes, he would feast on Daddy Twink's body, running his hands over the chiseled chest and stomach. Paris could imagine what it would be like to feel those hard muscles under that soft, silky skin.

Paris then would lean down close to the small rose-red nipple. Daddy Twink would tremble at the anticipation of his touch. Paris's right hand would slip down under the towel to find his hard, firm monster of a cock. Wrap his fingers around it, Paris would slowly stroke Daddy Twink. Paris would plant a soft

wet kiss on the tiny nipple, then circle his tongue around the nub.

A gasp would escape Daddy Twink. The sound would be so soft and quiet that only Paris could hear. He would feel it in the throb of the dick in his hand and the quivering of Daddy's Twink's body at his touch. They would be silent pleas to continue, to go faster, but Paris would take his time.

Paris would continue to slowly stroke Daddy Twink. He would begin to explore Daddy Twink's hard, defined body with his mouth, first moving to the hairless pit. Daddy Twink would jolt from the pleasure, then simmer down as Paris moved up to kiss the tight, bulging biceps.

Slowly gliding back down, Daddy Twink would tense with pleasure overload at the slow circles Paris would make in his pit. Paris would flick his tongue at the very moment he relaxed, sending Daddy Twink tugging at his bonds. He would get a reprieve when Paris moved his mouth back to the raised nipple.

Paris would graze his teeth over the tough skin. Daddy Twink's chest would be heaving, trying to catch his breath. Paris would continue his slow tease, moving to the other nipple. Like the first, he'd circle his tongue slowly around the nub. With his other hand, Paris would reach up and run a soothing hand over his nylon hood.

Once Daddy Twink's breathing became steady, Paris would move down, running his tongue through the deep valleys of Daddy Twink's muscles. He'd let out muffled grunts and groans punctuated with slight gasps whenever Paris found a sensitive spot.

Paris would be tempted to ravish these random spots, but his goal was the slab of meat coating his hand in sticky pre-cum as he slowly stroked.

The towel would slip off as Paris's tongue tour would venture down to Daddy Twink's groin. He would lick up from the thick base to the flared head. Daddy Twink's breath would hitch with anticipation, only to turn into a soft whimper of disappointment when Paris made his way back down.

Paris would then take the path down to Daddy Twink's balls that were simmering with the prospect of release. Taking one, then the other in his mouth, Daddy Twink's hips would rise with moaning pleas for release. Paris would not grant him that gift until he was done enjoying him.

Paris would move farther down Daddy Twink's body once he was done bathing his balls and had him breathing heavily with lust. Down his toned, powerful legs to his long toes that Paris would suckle one by one, giving Daddy Twink a chance to catch his breath before Paris began his next sexual attack.

Right as Daddy Twink's breath evened out, Paris would run his tongue in a zig-zag pattern over the sole. Daddy Twink would jerk and jolt from the slide of Paris's tongue over the obscure erogenous zone. He would not get a chance to recover before Paris moved to the other sole.

Paris would wait until the pleasure was unbearable to move to this foot's toes. Paris would look up along Daddy Twink's beautiful body, unable to see his face from his heaving chest. Moving up his leg, Paris

would take the colossal cock in his hand and resume slowly stroking it.

This time, when Paris ran his tongue up the rock-hard shaft, he'd run his tongue over the fat crown. He'd end the tease with a kiss, then wrap his lips over the tip, taking a moment to let Daddy Twink's flavor fill his mouth. Relenting to Daddy Twink's soft pleas for more, Paris would do his best to take in as much as possible.

Stretching his jaw to its limits, Paris would slowly swallow him down until Daddy Twink was pushing at the back of his throat. It would only be six or so inches because of how fat Daddy Twink's dick was. Paris would make up the rest with his stroking hands.

It would be slow going for the first minute or two, as Paris would need to adjust to the stretch of his jaw. Then Paris would be overcome with his own burning lust. He'd slurp Daddy Twink down, pushing at his limits to get more in. He'd try to get more of Daddy Twink down but only get another inch or so in his zeal.

Pulling off Daddy Twink, Paris would grab the lube and liberally drizzle it over his cock. With one hand coating Daddy Twink's length, he'd use his other hand to prep himself as best he could. With a brave determination, Paris would climb up on the table and straddle Daddy Twink. He'd look down at the faceless mask as he rose up and guided the humongous cock to his ass.

Closing his eyes and taking a deep breath, he'd lower himself onto Daddy Twink. He'd exhale slowly as he pressed Daddy Twink into him, forcing himself to stretch to accommodate the thick beast he was impaling himself on. He'd pause every so often to allow his body to adjust. After a few deep breaths, he'd continue feeding Daddy Twink's python into him.

It would seem like an eternity before Paris would bottom out with eight inches in him. Opening his eyes, he'd look at the mask, wishing he could see Daddy Twink's face. Slowly, he would raise and lower himself. He'd feel every thick inch throbbing in him with the need for release.

With the stretch shifting into pleasure, Paris would stroke himself in time with his thrusting hips. He would take it slow, dragging out his pleasure. Daddy Twink wouldn't be able to hold back. He would start bucking his hips up into Paris, bouncing him up and down. Paris would feel him going deeper and deeper into him.

Paris's hand would be flying along his seven inches. His balls would start tingling. Daddy Twink's pumps into him would grow faster and more urgent. Closing his eyes, Paris would grit his teeth. His body would tense with the surge exploding from his cock, speckling Daddy Twink's perfect abs in white.

The quivering and squeezing of Paris's body around Daddy Twink's cock would set Daddy Twink off. He'd buck madly into Paris. His cock would swell. Paris would lean back, arch his back. He'd feel it, the pulse of Daddy Twink's cock glazing his insides. Paris would jerk in time with the blasts.

Milking out the last drops of semen from his cock, Paris would open his eyes and take several deep breaths. He would look down with a satisfied smile at his cum covered cock, then up along Daddy Twink's

abs dripping in cum. He'd move up past those delicate nipples to Daddy Twink's masked face. Only the mask was gone.

Paris bolted up, wide-eyed. "Daniel!" he yelled. He looked down at his crotch. "Really?" Paris groaned when he realized he had soaked through his underwear into his pants from his private explosion. He fell back down onto the bed with a groan.

"You called?" Daniel asked, coming in the door. He looked at Paris's distraught face. "Are you okay?"

Closing his eyes, Paris said, "No." He looked at the blurry Daniel standing over him. "Could you wash my pants," he paused for a second before adding, "and my underwear?"

"Did you…?" Daniel hid his smirk with his hand. "Leave them on the bed while you go get cleaned up in the bathroom."

Paris squinted at Daniel, trying to bring him into focus. "Could you bring me my glasses and phone, please?"

"Here." Daniel pulled them from the pockets of his apron. "I grabbed them on my way."

Putting on his glasses, Paris started scrolling through the notifications. "I don't get these messages from Hunter and Mark. They're saying that Hunter's truck was stolen."

"His truck is right out front," Daniel responded, perplexed. "I'm parked behind him."

Setting his phone down, Paris sat up. "I need to." He stopped when he remembered his situation. "Would you mind?"

"Not at all. Strip," Daniel teased. "I'll step outside to make sure Hunter's truck is still there and then come back."

Paris felt a slight relief from his embarrassment. "Thank you."

CARLOS, BILLY, AND THE ATTACK TWINK

"**C**OULD THIS DAY get any worse?" Mark asked, storming through the front door. "Where is Paris?"

Hunter calmly shut the door behind them. "I'm sure he was busy. That's why he didn't answer our calls." Hunter pulled out his ringing phone. "Speak of the devil." Hunter put his phone to his ear. "Hey, Paris, we're home now. We'll see you in a minute." Hunter glanced at the notifications on his phone, then tucked it back in his pocket.

"I know it's not his fault I dropped my phone and cracked the screen." Mark turned and hugged Hunter. "Why didn't he call or text you?"

Hunter squeezed Mark tight. "Don't be mad, but he did. My phone went into driving mode. He's left me a couple dozen phone and text messages." Mark began squeezing Hunter. "Babe, you're hurting me. Babe."

"I really need to hit the gym and work out some of this stress." Mark let go of him. "Maybe get a massage." They both turned their heads toward the kitchen when they heard unintelligible yelling. "What now?"

Hunter and Mark stepped into the dining room to hear Daniel yell, "Get out of my kitchen! Both of you!" A moment later, Billy and Carlos came rushing out with an angry Daniel on their heels, brandishing a spatula. He pointed it at Carlos, who was hiding behind Mark. "If you want something to eat, I'll make it for you." He pointed the spoon at Billy, who was hiding behind Hunter. "Don't touch my chicken."

"When did you hire the attack twink?" Carlos asked.

Billy stuck his tongue out at Daniel. "Your chicken probably sucks anyway."

"I see you two have met Daniel." Mark laughed. "He's helping with the cooking and cleaning this week."

Hunter looked around. "Where's Paris?"

"He's, um, in one of the spare bedrooms, waiting for his pants," Daniel answered hesitantly. The buzz of the drier went off. "Sounds like they're dry."

Hunter raised an eyebrow. "Why are his pants in the drier?"

"He was helping me cook and spilled something on them," Daniel answered nervously.

Mark looked at Hunter, then at Daniel. "He could have put on one of our robes."

"I suggested that." Daniel shuffled his feet. "He didn't feel comfortable wearing a robe without any underwear."

After a prolonged awkward silence, Carlos spoke up. "Okay, if no one else is going to ask it, I will. Why isn't he wearing underwear?"

"It soaked through," Daniel answered, hoping they believed the lie. "I'm going to take him his clothes." Daniel turned to go back into the kitchen, then turned back to point the spatula at Carlos and Billy as he glared at them. "Keep them out of my kitchen."

Once he was sure Daniel was out of earshot, Billy said, "I'm going to fix his chicken."

"Nope." Hunter grabbed Billy by the collar as he tried to slip by. "No pissing off the person feeding us."

"Or has access to sharp knives," Daniel added as he strolled through with Paris's folded clothes.

Carlos looked at Mark. "He knows that's not funny with our history, right?

"Wasn't meant to be!" Daniel yelled back.

Billy looked up at Hunter questioningly. "Are he and Paris a thing?"

"No," Hunter answered.

Mark added, "Maybe."

"How did it happen?" Carlos asked excitedly. "Give us all the details."

Hunter rolled his eyes. "It didn't. Mark, please, don't encourage them. We have things to discuss."

"What's going on?" Billy asked.

Hunter looked at Mark, then at Billy and Carlos. "Sit down at the kitchen table. We'll talk about everything once Paris comes in."

"He'll be out in a minute," Daniel announced, walking back in. "He's a little embarrassed. If you guys don't mention it, I'll make you some sandwiches."

Carlos perked up. "We won't say a thing."

"Hold off on the sandwiches," Hunter jumped in. "I want you at this meeting, too. Where are Cody and Brad?"

Taking a seat at the kitchen table, Daniel answered, "They went to the house you rented to set up."

"We'll fill them in later, then." Hunter took a seat at the head of the table.

Mark sat on the other end. Billy and Carlos took seats across from Daniel. After a few minutes, Paris came rushing in, flustered. Everyone turned to look at him. He froze in the doorway, not knowing what to do. Mark saw Carlos nudge Billy when he was about to comment.

"Come sit down," Mark said sweetly. "We'll discuss why you didn't answer our calls later."

Paris took a timid step forward. "I'm sorry about that." He quickly rushed to the empty seat beside Daniel. "Um, why did you guys think Hunter's truck was stolen?"

Mark and Hunter locked eyes, silently arguing about who should tell the story. Mark spoke up. "We—"

"You," Hunter corrected.

Mark nodded at Hunter. "Correction, I was a little distraught after what happened at the caterer, and when we left the coffeehouse, we were looking for Hunter's truck instead of my car."

"The police were not amused," Hunter groaned.

Mark pulled his cracked phone out and sat it in front of Paris. "I dropped my phone and cracked the screen."

73

"I'll get it repaired right away." Paris then asked, "Why do we need a new caterer?"

Mark waved his hand at the other end of the table. "Hunter?"

"Our caterer died," Hunter said solemnly. "When we got to his shop, there were police, and we saw them take his body out."

Daniel's eyes grew wide. "Michael's dead?" Everyone looked at him. "I work as a cater waiter for him. I was actually scheduled to work at your wedding."

"How were you going to work the wedding and be Paris's date?" Billy's question was followed by Carlos's elbow into his side. "Ouch!"

Confused, Paris asked Billy, "Why would Daniel be my date?"

"I need to call his husband, Michael." Daniel got up. "If you'll excuse me."

Once he had left the room, Carlos said, "Wait. Your dead caterer was named Michael and married a man named Michael?"

"Apparently." Hunter shrugged. "That's one way to make sure you don't call out the wrong name in bed."

Paris began massaging the bridge of his nose. "Do you know how long it took me to find M and M Catering for you?"

"I know." Mark reached out and patted Paris's hand. "Tell them the rest, Hunter."

Hunter shook his head slightly. "Mark thinks Daddy Twink is responsible for killing our caterer."

"Daniel?" Billy asked, perplexed.

Hunter returned the confused look. "No. Daddy Twink is this guy that produces fan content. He hides his face in all the videos, so no one knows who he is."

"Why would you think Daniel is Daddy Twink?" Mark asked.

Billy answered simply, "He's obviously a daddy."

"And a twink," Carlos finished.

Carlos and Billy looked at each other before saying, "Daddy Twink," in unison.

"Wait. Can a twink be a daddy?" Carlos pondered.

"He's not Daddy Twink," Paris blurted out. "Daddy Twink responded to my message. He was trying to get an audition. He chose his words poorly."

Billy scratched his head. "Wait. Are you in a throple with Daddy Twink and Daniel?"

"I'm not dating anyone. Why would you think…" Paris put a hand up at Billy. "You know what? I don't care. When do your boyfriends get here so you can be their problem?"

Carlos and Billy shared a look before Carlos spoke. "They won't be here until the day of the wedding."

"Jordan has some super-secret project to do that he won't tell me about," Billy grumbled. "I even tried to bribe him with fried chicken." Billy yelled at Daniel in the next room, "Real fried chicken!"

Daniel came in from the kitchen waving a spatula at Billy. "Talk bad about my cooking again, and I will make you my bitch."

"Um, is he serious?" Billy asked, wide-eyed.

Mark laughed. "Yes, and I'll enjoy watching him do it."

75

Daniel's face softened when he looked at Hunter. "Michael had a heart attack."

"So it wasn't Daddy Twink," Hunter said, looking directly at Mark.

You could hear the confusion in Daniel's voice when he asked, "Why would it be Daddy Twink?"

"No reason." Hunter turned his attention to Paris. "We'd like to set up a meeting with Daddy Twink, so we can clear the air."

Paris pulled out his phone and started looking through the calendar. "You guys have a packed schedule this week with shooting and the wedding."

"Make it happen," Mark growled, angrier than he intended. He took the bite out of his voice before saying, "Move what you need around. We'll help you find a new caterer."

Returning to his seat, Daniel said, "Don't find a new caterer yet. Let me find out from Michael what he's going to do about the catering jobs."

"Twenty-four hours," Hunter responded. "In the meantime, we're going to institute some new rules for this week." He looked at Mark, who gave him the nod to go ahead. "No one leaves the house alone. Everyone shares their location on their phones with everyone else. No pranks or surprises. Too many odd things are happening, and I will not have our wedding ruined."

Puzzled, Carlos asked, "Because the caterer had a heart attack?"

"It's complicated," Mark answered.

Hunter snorted. "Not that complicated. Anyway, that's everything."

"Tell him." Daniel nudged Paris.

Paris found everyone staring at him. "No."

"Tell him," Daniel insisted.

Paris glared at Daniel. "Now is not the time."

"Will you tell me already?" Hunter sighed. "What terrible thing has happened now?"

Paris turned his attention to Hunter. "Nothing bad. It's about this project with Luscious Lexi. It can wait."

"Tell him." Daniel nudged him again.

Paris glared back at Daniel. "Not now."

"Why not?" Daniel argued.

Hunter put his face in his hands. "Would the happy couple please stop fighting and tell me already?"

"So they are dating!" Billy blurted out.

Paris and Daniel both shouted back, "We're not dating!"

"Paris, will you ... please ... tell me already?" Hunter groaned.

Paris took a moment to compose himself. "It's the project with Luscious Lexi. I don't think you should do it."

"What?!" Billy shouted.

Carlos followed it with, "Why?!"

Hunter held up a hand for the two to settle down, then asked calmly, "Paris, please explain."

"Well..." Paris looked to Daniel for support. He gave Paris a reassuring smile. Turning back to Hunter, Paris nervously said, "It makes more sense for me to run it for you."

Hunter motioned with his hand to Paris. "Go on."

"You have all the experience and connections with the adult film industry, and you're in the middle of

77

rebranding your studio." Paris felt Daniel give his knee a squeeze. "You need to put all your attention into that. This venture is risky and requires a lot of time, and I can give it that time, that is, if you don't need me here, I mean."

Mark reached out and patted Paris's hand. "I made that same argument today, and Hunter agreed."

"Really?" Paris asked, bright-eyed.

Hunter chuckled. "Yes, which means you'll be working with these two more." He pointed at Billy and Carlos. "Good luck."

"Fuck you." Billy stuck his tongue out at Hunter.

"No, you're fucking me tomorrow." Mark thought for a moment. "Or is it Billy?"

PEPPERMINT LOTION

PARIS PAUSED BEFORE turning the key to his apartment. Turning around, he said, "You didn't need to walk me to my door."

"Maybe I wanted to," Daniel answered smugly. "Mark and Hunter said no one goes anywhere alone."

Paris turned and opened the door. "Don't remind me. Billy tried to follow me into the bathroom."

"He and Carlos are filming tomorrow, so they'll be out of our hair," Daniel commented.

Paris stepped into his apartment, then turned around to face Daniel. "Okay, I'm home. You can go now."

"You're not even going to ask me in?" Daniel asked with mock hurt.

Paris rolled his eyes. "You're one of those annoying friends that likes to hang out, aren't you?"

"Yes." Daniel beamed proudly. "I also have something to run by you, so can I come in?"

Paris stepped aside and gestured him in. He pretended to be annoyed by Daniel's intrusion when he was happy to have the company. He rarely had a guest that wasn't a random hookup. Even that hadn't happened since he went into full wedding planning mode three months ago.

He watched Daniel take in his luxury apartment. Shutting the door, he said, "Have a seat."

"Man, you have all this to yourself?" Daniel asked, turning around. "Hunter and Mark are really overpaying you. Do you think I could get a raise?"

Paris felt a twinge of guilt when he said, "I couldn't afford this on what they pay me."

"Oh." Daniel looked at him questioningly. "Your parents?"

Paris took his glasses off and pretended to clean them. "No. My own money." He felt a bit guilty, like he was rubbing Daniel's nose in his wealth. Slipping his glasses back on, he asked, "Can I get you something to drink? I have red and white wine."

"Water is fine." Daniel sat down on the couch. "You have a really nice place."

Paris handed Daniel his water before sitting down. "Thanks. I can't wait to see your place."

"That might scare you." Daniel laughed. "There's four of us living in a two-bedroom apartment."

Paris's eyes grew wide. "Four of you in a two-bedroom apartment?"

"It's not that big of a deal. I have my own room. The other three are in a throple and share the big bedroom." Daniel snapped his fingers. "You met one of my roommates, Terry, the barista from Grind House. "

Paris thought for a moment. "You know, he looked familiar."

"Probably from Grind House." Daniel shrugged.

Paris shook his head. "No, that was the first time I've been there."

"He does have one of those faces." Daniel brushed it off.

Paris thought about it as he took a drink of water. "Okay, so what did you want to run by me?"

"Keep an open mind." Daniel sat his glass on the coffee table. "I talked to Michael, and he can't afford to give Hunter and Mark a refund. All the food has already been ordered."

Paris grew suspicious. "Okay."

"I've seen the menu. It's really simple," Daniel began.

Paris held up a hand to stop him. "No. I know what you're about to say, and the answer is no."

"Come on, Paris, I can do this. I know I can." Daniel continued, "It'll save you from having to try and find someone to cater, which you probably won't be able to do."

Paris mauled over his words. "I hate that you're right. For the sake of my sanity, I'm going to tell them Michael found a replacement cook."

"Technically, he did." He winked at Paris. "Daniel, to your rescue again."

Paris forced himself not to smile. "Yes, Daddy Daniel to my rescue again."

"Daddy Daniel." He laughed. "Better than Daddy Twink?"

Paris fell back against the couch in annoyance. "He hasn't responded to my request about meeting Mark

and Hunter. What's worse is that he turned his messages off right after that."

"That sucks, but if Hunter and Mark aren't going to hire him, why do they want to meet him?" Daniel asked.

Paris groaned. "Mark's being paranoid. He and Hunter are the only ones in their group that haven't had some encounter with a crazy psychopath. That note from Daddy Twink kind of set him off."

"Didn't Daddy Twink send you a message saying all he wanted was an audition?" Daniel commented.

Paris turned his head to look at Daniel. "Then someone almost ran Mark and Hunter over, then the caterer died, and then they thought someone stole Hunter's truck."

"He didn't have anything to do with the first two, and no one stole Hunter's truck. They forgot they took Mark's car," Daniel argued.

Paris let out a defeated laugh. "I've learned that you don't argue with crazy."

"True." Daniel studied Paris for a moment. "You look stressed."

Paris sighed. "I am."

"Come on." Daniel patted Paris's knee. "Take me to your bedroom, and I'll give you a massage."

Paris looked at Daniel in disbelief. "You know that's how all the old adult films start, right?"

"Yes, but don't worry. You're keeping your cute little black briefs on." Daniel patted Paris's knee again, then got up. "Come on, show me what lotions you have." Daniel stuck out his hand for Paris.

Paris took the offered hand and let himself be pulled up. "How do you know I have lotions? Because I'm rich?"

"No, because you're gay," Daniel teased. "Lead the way."

"Follow me," Paris relented. "How are you going to keep from getting lotion all over your clothes?"

Nonchalantly, Daniel said, "I'll strip down to my boxers. Please, try to control yourself."

"Control myself?" Paris turned around and bumped into Daniel.

Daniel retorted, "Yeah, in two days, I've had to do laundry for you because of your personal detonations."

"Yeah, I've got to remember to bring an extra set of clothes for tomorrow." Paris blushed.

Daniel took Paris by the shoulders and spun him around. "And deny me the opportunity to wash your underwear?"

"Fuck you," Paris grunted, stepping into his bedroom. "My lotions are in the bathroom over there."

Daniel clapped his hands together, then rubbed them. "Great. Strip to your itsy-bitsy bikini briefs and lay face down on the bed."

"I can't believe I'm letting you do this," Paris groaned, setting his glasses on the nightstand.

"Me, either," Daniel remarked from the bathroom. "Any preference on a scent?"

Paris pulled his shirt off and folded it neatly. He noticed Daniel shut the bathroom door to give him privacy. "Whatever you think is best."

"Choices." Daniel called back, "Just yell when you're ready."

Paris undressed, trying to push away the memory of the half dream, half fantasy he had earlier, where he looked into Daddy Twink's face and saw Daniel's instead. Setting his folded clothes on the nightstand, he wondered what that meant and why he remembered it now.

Getting on the bed, he lay with his head facing away from the bathroom door. Nervously he called out, "Ready."

"I'm going to turn the lights off and leave the bathroom light on," Daniel said soothingly. "All I want you to do is lie there and relax."

Paris tried to dispel his foolish nervousness with a deep breath. "Okay," he said with a slow exhale.

The lights went out, then Paris felt the bed shift. "Close your eyes. Let me do all the work." Paris obeyed, trying not to be startled when Daniel straddled him and he felt Daniel's bare skin against his. "Just relax."

Needing to distract himself from Daniel's touch, Paris asked, "What scent did you choose?"

"Peppermint. You're going to smell like a candy cane when I'm done." Paris jumped when he felt the cold cream hit his back. Daniel laughed. "Sorry, I meant to warn you. Let me know if I'm too rough or too soft. I want it to be just right for you."

Paris felt Daniel's hands move the lotion over his back, then come back down to his waist. Daniel had his thumbs on either side of his spine, then slowly moved them up Paris's back, applying just the right amount of pressure. Paris groaned at the release of pent-up stress from his muscles.

"Good?" Daniel asked, running his fingers along Paris's shoulder blades. "I'm not hurting you, am I?"

Paris gasped when he felt Daniel release a knot in his back. "Fantastic," he purred. "You should do this professionally."

"I did, for about six months." Daniel began working his fingers into Paris's shoulders. "Before you ask, I stopped doing massage after the place I worked at was raided for giving happy endings." Daniel tapped his fingertips down to the base of Paris's back. "I was lucky enough not to be there that day. I was supposed to be, but I was too hungover to come in."

Paris swallowed hard before he asked, "Did you ever, you know, um…"

"Give happy endings?" Daniel began working on Paris's left side. "Oh, yeah. The guy I was dating got me the job."

Paris grunted at the release of more tension from his body. "Your boyfriend got you a job having sex with other men?"

"I was eye candy to him. A trophy he wanted to put on display for his friends." Daniel began working on the other side. "He was a bankroll to me, paying all my bills. Buying me clothes and giving me money to go out."

Paris hesitantly asked, "What happened?"

"I went out one night with my friends. We came back to his place for an after-party. I passed out in the living room." Daniel began working his way back up Paris's back. "I woke up thinking my friends had gone, so I went to bed. That's where I found them. Spit roasting my boyfriend."

Paris asked, "Were you mad?"

"Not at first. I went to the guest room and passed out." Daniel worked the tight muscles in Paris's left arm. "The next morning, when I woke up, I overheard them in the kitchen saying nasty things about me. Then my boyfriend asked if they would like to take my place."

Paris could tell Daniel was hiding the hurt. "What happened then?"

"Three days later, I broke up with him and started dating one of his buddies." Daniel moved to Paris's other arm. "When he was tired of me, I moved to the next guy. Then the next. I had, I think, fifteen boyfriends in a year." Paris couldn't believe what he was hearing. "I'm not really sure because I was drunk most of the time, and some guys I just hooked up with and didn't leave until they kicked me out."

Paris felt the need to ask, "What happened? You've obviously got your act together now."

"I hit rock bottom." Daniel ran his hands up and down Paris's arms. "I ran through all the rich gays. None of the young party gays wanted anything to do with me. My parents wouldn't let me move back home. I was homeless." He patted Paris's back. "All done. Next time you do me."

Paris rolled over under Daniel. Looking up at Daniel's face, he repeated, "What happened?"

"I couch and bed hopped until I met a nice guy. Oddly enough, I met him on the apps. We only hooked up the first time I met him." Daniel took a deep breath and closed his eyes. "I didn't trust him at first. He'd always find me on the apps, no matter what screen name I used. Asked me if I needed a place. Of course, I did. The thing was, he didn't allow alcohol or drugs in his place. He was sober."

Through the dim light, Paris saw tears in Daniel's eyes. "It was a cold winter, and no one was willing to put me up, so I finally took him up on his offer." Daniel laughed a humorless laugh. "That was the winter we all got snowed in for four days."

"I remember that." Paris took Daniel's hands and held them. "You don't have to—"

Daniel put two fingers to Paris's lips to silence him. "For the first time in over a year, I didn't have a drink in twenty-four hours or a hangover. He made me soup, and we watched *Golden Girls* reruns. By day three, I didn't want to leave, and I didn't."

"How long were you with him?" Paris asked guiltily, "Was he your boyfriend?"

Daniel took Paris's hands. "No. He became the gay father I needed, though. I lived with him for almost two years, getting my life together. I got a job. Started going to the gym. He taught me to love myself. He was the first person that didn't want anything from me but for me to be happy."

"What happened to him?" Paris asked, knowing the answer in his heart.

"He died in a car accident." Daniel squeezed Paris's hands, then let go. "I should go." Daniel moved off of Paris and the bed. "It's getting late."

Paris reached out and grabbed Daniel's hand. "It is late. Why don't you stay here? You can get up early and head out in the morning." Daniel looked at Paris's hand holding his. "I have an extra toothbrush." Seeing

the pain in Daniel's eyes, he added, "You're in no shape to drive."

"Okay," Daniel answered softly.

They didn't say anything unnecessary after that. Paris opened the bed while Daniel used his shower. When Paris came out of the shower, Daniel was already in bed, curled up in a ball on his side with his back to the bathroom door. Paris knew he wasn't asleep, but he let Daniel pretend.

Turning the bathroom light off, the room fell into darkness. Paris slipped into the bed. Putting his glasses on the nightstand, he turned on his side so his back was to Daniel. After the longest thirty seconds of his life, Paris flipped over and spooned Daniel. He felt Daniel tense up at his touch.

Paris whispered softly to him, "I'm going to hold you until you fall asleep, if that's okay."

"Yes." Daniel interlaced his fingers with Paris's. "Thank you."

I'M NOT LETTING YOU GO

MARK STOOD THERE, resisting the urge to throttle the young man standing uncomfortably before him. He couldn't deny the remorse carved into the young man's face. The fact that Caleb was making him do this didn't discount the genuine regret the boy felt about almost hitting Mark with his car.

"I truly am sorry," the muscled boy said. "I should have been paying attention, and not in such a rush. I hope you can accept my apology."

Mark briefly looked at Hunter and Caleb, who stood behind the boy with imploring eyes. "You know you could have killed us." Mark hated the fatherly way his words came out.

"Yes, sir." It was obvious the muscled boy was forcing himself to look Mark in the eye. "I should have known better since I'm majoring in criminal justice."

Mark cut his eyes at Caleb before looking back at the nervous, muscled boy. "Okay, I forgive you. I want you to be careful from now on, and, oh, my God, I sound like my father, and I don't even have children!"

"Come on, Todd." Caleb stepped up and put a hand on the muscled boy's shoulder. "Let's get out of here before you end up in one of their movies."

Hunter waited for the two to leave to step up to Mark. "Do you feel better now?"

"Yes," Mark grumbled. "And no. I have this feeling that something is going to ruin our wedding."

Hunter pulled him into a hug. "Nothing is going to ruin our marriage. We are getting married in less than a week. Paris said Michael found a new chef to cook for the reception. We already have your best man here, the flower boy, and Dennis and Benjamin will be here Friday."

"Did we tell Carlos he's going to be the flower boy, and that Jordan is really the ring bearer?" Mark asked, laughing into Hunter's chest.

Hunter's body shook with laughter. "I don't think he'll mind." Hunter gave Mark a big squeeze. "Now, I want you to put all those bad thoughts out of your head. You should be some groomzilla right now."

"I'm sorry. I don't want you to think I'm getting cold feet." Mark snuggled into Hunter's chest. "We missed out on so much time together. Things are going great for us, but I can't shake this feeling that something is going to ruin it."

Hunter rubbed Mark's back soothingly. "Nothing is going to ruin our wedding. Paris wouldn't let it. I wouldn't let it. I let you slip through my fingers once. I'm never going to let that happen again. It's me and you, buddy, forever and always. You got that?"

"Yes." Mark gave Hunter a kiss. "For the record, I'm not letting you let me go. I don't need a ceremony or a ring to know that you're always going to be mine, and I'm always going to be yours. We were meant to be."

Hunter ran a hand through Mark's hand. "I'm looking forward to our first dance with you as my husband. I know it sounds silly, but that is the moment I'm looking forward to."

"Me too." Mark laid his head back against Hunter's chest. "I know we joke about sex all the time, but the only man I really want in my bed is you."

Hunter patted Mark on the ass. "Good. Now let's go find Carlos so he can fuck you. Good thing it's on a desk and not a bed."

"You're such an ass." Mark laughed.

Hunter kissed the top of his head. "I'm your ass, and I'm also your director. Now let's get it in gear. We're losing daylight."

"We're filming indoors." Mark sighed. "Let me just enjoy this moment a little longer. I love being held by you."

Hunter tightened his arms around Mark. "I love waking up with you spooning me every morning."

"I do, too," Mark said with a smile. "I do, too."

BLOW JOB OR A SANDWICH

"**Y**OU CAN'T DO this to us!" Paris shouted into his phone as he walked into his office. "The wedding is next week!" He saw Daniel poke his head in. "Oh, you will be refunding our money! You don't know who you're messing with, asshole. Goodbye!" Paris hung up the phone, then shouted angrily, "That motherfucker!"

Daniel moved to Paris's side. "Is everything okay?" Paris looked at him with angry, wet eyes. "You're shaking." He pulled Paris into a hug. "Let it out. I'm here."

"That bastard we hired to officiate the wedding is backing out and saying he won't refund us our money." Paris blurted out in one breath. Putting his arms around Daniel, he continued. "He says it's against his religious beliefs to officiate a same-sex marriage." Paris snarled, "It wasn't against his fucking religious beliefs when he cashed the check."

Daniel gasped. "Paris, you're hurting me."

"I'm sorry!" Paris immediately let go, but Daniel held on.

Daniel laughed. "I'm kidding."

"You ass." Paris struggled in Daniel's arms. "Let go."

Daniel tightened the hug. "When you tell me where that rage monster you just unleashed came from."

"That wasn't a rage monster." Paris continued struggling in Daniel's grip. "Let go."

They struggled and laughed for a bit; when they locked eyes, Daniel quickly let go. Uncomfortably he said, "Hunter wanted me to remind you that you have a video call with Lexi Luscious at ten." Daniel checked the time on his phone. "Which is in ten minutes."

"I can't meet her looking like this!" Paris panicked. "I bet my eyes are all red, and my face is all flush!"

Daniel took Paris by the shoulders. "Go wash your face. I'll turn your computer on, then I'll make your morning coffee for you."

"Okay." Paris nodded. He turned away from Daniel, then back. He had the urge to kiss Daniel, but instead, he said, "Thank you." He rushed off to the bathroom to clean himself up. *That was a moment back there, wasn't it?* He took off his glasses, then splashed water on his face.

Drying his face off, he slipped his glasses back on and took a long, hard look at himself in the mirror. *I was imagining it. I was in my underwear, and he was in his boxers with me all night, and nothing happened.* Paris shook the thoughts away, then rushed back to his office.

Sitting down, he began logging into his email. Finding the link to his meeting in his email, he clicked

it. He adjusted his camera to make sure Lexi would be able to see him properly. He took a cleansing breath, then joined the meeting. He watched the words "Establishing Connection" flash on the screen.

"You've got three minutes still," Daniel said, setting his coffee down on the desk. "Exactly how you like it. One spoon of monk fruit, a splash of almond milk, and piping hot."

Paris looked over his shoulder at Daniel. "Thank you. Daddy Daniel to the rescue again."

"Believe it. Daddy has your back," Daniel teased before walking away.

"He's your daddy?" The feminine voice that spoke startled Paris. He looked at his screen to see the deceivingly dainty Lexi Luscious grinning at him. "As far as daddies go, he's definitely a hot one, if not a little small."

Wide-eyed, Paris sputtered out, "He's not my daddy. I mean, he's helped me out with some problems, and last night we slept together, but we didn't have sex—"

"We're just friends," Daniel said, clamping a hand over Paris's mouth. "I'm going to season the roast and put it in the slow cooker for dinner." He directed his words to Paris. "Are you going to be normal now?" Paris nodded his head. Daniel removed his hand, then looked into the web camera. "He's all yours."

Horrified, Paris looked at the screen to see an amused Lexi staring back at him. His aghast wasn't eased when Lexi playfully said, "Your daddy cooks for you. Better not let him slip away."

"Never let your boy leave hungry or horny!" Daniel yelled from the kitchen. "Somewhere out there is someone willing to give him a blowjob and a sandwich!"

Paris's eyes grew as wide as saucers. Stunned, he said, "I can't believe he said that."

"A little advice," Lexi said, trying to contain her laughter. "Snap him up before someone else offers him a blow job or a sandwich." Paris gawked at her. "Now, on to business. You've impressed Hunter and Mark. Now dazzle me."

After fifteen minutes of spouting out numbers and figures, Paris could see that she was getting bored. She wasn't obvious about it. Truth be told, Paris was boring himself. He locked his phone with his notes and set it aside. He knew what he needed to do.

She said to dazzle her. Paris cleared his throat. "The truth is, the idea is great. You have a ton of great show ideas, but you have just as many bad ones. You need to be selective about what shows you make and really stand behind them."

Out of the corner of his eye, he saw Daniel moving about. "One thing you're missing is a really good cooking show. Maybe a shirtless muscle twink showing people how to cook. People will watch it to learn to cook and ogle the hot chef."

"Interesting idea." Lexi leaned into the camera. "Did you have someone in mind for the show?"

Paris smiled proudly. "He's cooking in the kitchen right now."

"I love the idea. He is hot. Funny, too." Lexi lowered her voice conspiratorially. "He doesn't know yet, does he?"

Paris chuckled softly. "Not yet."

Lexi leaned back away from the camera. "I like you. You have vision, and your balls are almost as big as mine. Metaphorically speaking, that is. I'm going to like working with you. After the wedding, send me a test show to watch."

"The wedding." Paris moaned in despair. "I'm going to be glad when it's over. If it's not one thing, it's another. Now I've got to find a replacement to officiate the wedding."

"Daddy Twink again?" Lexi's question caught Paris off guard.

"No, no. At least, I don't think so." Perplexed, Paris asked, "How do you know about Daddy Twink?" He knew the answer by the look she gave him. "Mark."

She nodded. "Well, I'm bringing Ryan from Walden Woods with me. He's a wedding officiant. Since we reopened, it's been a popular wedding spot. He's done at least thirty weddings."

"Do you think he'll do it?" Paris asked eagerly.

Lexi fluttered her hands. "He loves doing weddings. Try to stop him."

"Catastrophe averted again." Paris fell back into his chair. "Thank you."

Lexi smiled sweetly. "You're welcome." Changing the subject, she asked, "Who is this Daddy Twink? He intrigues me. Are his videos any good? I haven't subscribed yet, but they look interesting."

"They are hot," Paris admitted. "It was the note he left with his audition video that set Mark off."

"Well, if you find a way to contact him, I'd love to meet him," Lexi commented. "Good performers are hard to find."

Paris shook his head. "He turned his messages off again, but if I do get a hold of him, I'll let you know."

"Perfect. I have to go. I'll see you in a few days." Lexi paused. "Oh, and if you don't snatch that twinkie daddy up before I get there with Ryan, you may just lose him. Bye!"

Paris sat there a moment, looking at the blank video screen. He closed the app and listened to the sound of Daniel puttering around in the kitchen. He thought about their moment earlier, Daniel's embarrassing comment, and Lexi's advice. For a brief second, he allowed himself the fantasy of being Daniel's boyfriend.

Paris laughed to himself. *He's going to be so pissed I volunteered him for a show.*

MEETING WITH THE PROFESSOR PART 1

MARK SAT BEHIND the desk in the office in the rented home. Filtered sunlight from the window behind him cast the room in a warm glow. With the shelves lined with books and the scholarly knickknacks, Mark felt the part of a professor with his white button-down and tight khakis.

He tapped away at the keys on the laptop in front of him, pretending to be doing something important and scholarly. In reality, it was just a random Word document they had loaded that had a bunch of gibberish on the screen. He knew all eyes were on him, but pretended they didn't exist.

He looked up from the screen when Carlos's scripted knock on the door came. "Come in," Mark yelled. When the door opened, he stood and said, "Awe, Carlos, thanks for coming by. Please, have a seat."

"Is there something you wanted, Professor Mark?" Carlos asked, shutting the door behind him. He sat down with his legs spread wide.

Mark moved around the desk. Carlos looked different than he had when they first met a year ago. He'd put on some muscle that pulled the graphic on his t-shirt tight against him, and his biceps strained against the sleeves. His shorts were almost skin tight against his firm hard thighs and tapered out to sculpted grapefruit calf muscles that Mark envied.

Coming around the desk, Mark said, "It's about you and Billy."

"Him," Carlos groaned, annoyed. "What did he say I did this time?"

Leaning back on the desk, Mark said, "The two of you have been a disruption in my class. I need it to stop." Mark moved his hands to grip the edge of the desk. "I know he baits you. The next time he does, I don't want you to react. Be the bigger man."

"I am the bigger man." Carlos smirked, grabbing his crotch. "Way bigger."

Flustered, Mark said, "That's not what I meant." He knocked the strategically placed cup of pens off the desk. "One minute, please." Mark bent over and started picking up the pens, knowing the camera was getting close-ups of Carlos licking his lips as he ogled Mark's ass.

Carlos watched him fumble about gathering the pens, then set them back on the desk. Turning back to face Carlos, Mark asked, "Do you think you can do that for me?"

99

"That's asking a lot of me, Professor Mark." Carlos gave him a cocky smirk. "I'd need some way to release all that pent-up hostility." Carlos stood and moved close to Mark. "Maybe you could," Carlos licked his lips, "help me."

Uncomfortably, Mark said, "Carlos, what are you doing?"

"Come on, Professor." Carlos pressed his body against Mark. "You know you're the hottest professor on campus." Carlos put his left hand on the desk while his right hand reached around to cup Mark's ass. "If you want peace in your class, you need to give me a piece."

Mark swallowed, then sputtered out nervously, "Carlos, you're my student. I could get into a lot of trouble if anyone found out."

"If anyone asks, we'll tell them you're tutoring me privately." Carlos crushed his mouth to Mark's.

Mark kissed him back. The kiss was raw and hungry with their pent-up urges. Mark moved his hands from the desk to cup Carlos's plump yet firm ass. Carlos pulled Mark hard against him. Mark felt the young man's firmness pressing into him. Mark's hard cock throbbed with desire at the feel of Carlos grinding his hips into him.

Carlos stepped back, allowing Mark to drop to his knees. He popped open Carlos's shorts, then tugged them down, allowing Carlos's huge uncut cock to swing free. Mark took hold of the ten-inch flesh beast and stroked him. Mark watched Carlos's foreskin slide back and forth. Pre-cum glistened over the crown. Mark's mouth watered with anticipation. This was one of Mark's secret joys, sucking an uncut cock. So few in the industry had them.

Mark was brought back into the moment when Carlos cockily asked, "Are you going to suck me or what?"

Mark covered Carlos's tip with his mouth. Slipping his tongue into his foreskin, he swirled his tongue around. Carlos moaned. Mark swiped his tongue over the crown, then continued his trek along Carlos's swollen shaft. He took Carlos down about seven or so inches before he started to gag.

"Come on, Professor, you can do better than that." Carlos put a hand on the back of Mark's head. Miraculously, Mark swallowed down the rest. "That's it, take it all." With his hand resting on the back of Mark's head, Carlos let him do what he did best. Suck cock. "Fuck, yeah, suck it," Carlos growled as Mark worked his way back and forth along the length of his cock. "Damn, Professor, you got one hot mouth. I may need to pay you a few more visits after hours."

Carlos pulled Mark back up to his feet. His shirt came up and off. He kissed Mark savagely. He fumbled with the buttons on Mark's dress shirt. Growling in frustration, Carlos pulled the shirt open, sending buttons flying everywhere. He yanked Mark's dress shirt halfway down his arms, virtually immobilizing him.

"Carlos," Mark managed to pant out when Carlos moved down to his chest and started flicking his tongue over Mark's nipple. "Oh, fuck, Carlos." Carlos popped open the top of Mark's khakis. Lowering the zipper, Carlos shoved his hand down Mark's pants

and rubbed his straining hard-on through the white cotton briefs.

Carlos stood. Mark saw a fiery passion in his eyes. Mark took the opportunity to kick off his shoes. "Time for me to earn that A in your class, Professor." Carlos pulled Mark's hips forward by the waist of his pants, then shoved them with his underwear down his thick thighs.

Carlos dropped down to his knees and sucked Mark's seven-inch cock down with a sexual eagerness he hadn't expected. Mark felt Carlos's tongue swirling around his cock as he bobbed on Mark's cock. All the while, he was pulling Mark's pants farther down until they were bunched up around his ankles.

Mark held onto the desk, virtually tied up in his own clothing. The original idea was for Carlos to be the aggressor, but this wasn't part of the plan. Carlos was definitely going off-script, and he hoped Hunter loved it as much as he did. Considering Hunter hadn't stopped the scene yet, Mark guessed he did.

Carlos was back on his feet, kissing Mark again. He freed Mark's arms from his shirt and spun Mark around so he was trapped between him and the desk. Carlos growled in Mark's ear, "Time for some extra credit."

Carlos bent Mark over the desk. He was down behind Mark. He spread Mark's muscled ass, then dove in with his tornado tongue. Mark grabbed the other end of the desk. "Eat my hole, man," Mark purred in delight. "Fuck, you can have more than an A if you keep that up, my God!" Mark's eyes rolled

back in his head when he felt the rapid tap of Carlos's tongue against his pucker.

Behind him, Carlos stood. Toeing off his shoes, he dropped his shorts and stepped out of them. Tapping his cock on Mark's ass, Carlos let loose the cheesy line, "Time to give you the biggest D you've ever had, Professor."

Mark inhaled deeply, thankful he had used a butt plug earlier in anticipation of this event. Carlos pushed his cock head into Mark. There was a moment of resistance before Mark's ass welcomed Carlos in willingly. Mark slowly exhaled as Carlos slowly glided in. Mark was grateful, not for the first time in his career, that he knew how to take big dicks because of his well-endowed boyfriend.

"Yeah, I knew with a fat ass like that, you'd know how to take dick," Carlos snarled. He held onto Mark's hips and began thrusting mercilessly into Mark.

Mark arched his back and shoved his ass back into Carlos. "That feels so good. Damn. Fuck me! Fuck me!"

"I'm going to fuck this sweet ass every chance I get." Carlos pulled out suddenly. He pulled Mark off the desk, spun him around, and then pushed him back down onto the desk. "I want to see your face while I fuck you."

Carlos lifted Mark's legs up. He made quick work of the bunched-up pants and underwear, then pulled Mark to the edge of the desk. With Mark's legs resting on his shoulders, Carlos slammed back into Mark so hard that Mark had to grip the edge of the desk to keep from being flung off. Carlos's right

hand gripped Mark's hard cock. He jerked Mark as he fucked him.

"Carlos, yes! Fuck, yes!" Mark called out.

Carlos's hips rabbited forward with twenty or so short thrusts, then came a long slow pull out and hard slam in. Twenty more short thrusts, then two long slow pulls with hard slams. Mark knew Carlos was playing with him, dragging out the inevitable because he wanted to make sure Hunter got every shot and angle he needed from this moment.

Carlos suddenly pulled out and began rapidly pumping his cock. "I'm going to cum!" Carlos announced a split second before his hot white cream shot across Mark's cock and chest. Carlos's body tensed with the reverberation of the orgasm. He stepped back a moment but still held Mark's legs on his shoulders. "Fuck."

Mark went into action. Using Carlos's spunk as lube, he jerked his own cock. Carlos shoved two wiggling fingers into Mark's battered hole. Mark arched up, shouting, "I'm cumming!" White fluid was launched up into the air, splattering Mark, the desk, and probably the floor behind him. "Fuck! Fuck! Fuck!" he yelled as pulse after pulse exploded in him.

When Mark's orgasm finally subsided, Carlos pulled his fingers out and let Mark's legs down. "Does this mean I get an A in the course?" Carlos asked cockily.

Trying to catch his breath, Mark said, "For the day. I think you need some intense personal tutoring with me to maintain that A."

YOU'RE WITH FAMILY NOW

OUT OF BREATH and covered in spunk, Mark looked up from the desk at Carlos. "Pent up?"

"Yeah, you could say that." Carlos laughed it off. "Sorry about that."

Hunter tossed towels to Carlos and Mark. "I would say. Not quite what I imagined, but it worked, and it was hot as Hell."

"We don't need a reshoot?" Carlos asked hopefully as he wiped himself off.

Sitting up, Mark offered, "I'm perfectly okay with that. Just give me an hour to recover."

"No, we're good." Hunter looked over at Cody and Brad. "You boys can take five."

Carlos slipped on his shorts. "We can use the shower here, right?"

"Yes," Mark answered, getting off the desk. Still wiping himself off, he commented, "I don't know who shot more. Me or you."

Billy snickered. "Considering he hasn't had sex in two weeks, my money is on Carlos."

"Shut up, Billy," Carlos said through clenched teeth.

Setting the towel aside, Mark patted the spot on the desk next to him. "Now, just because I don't play your father in adult films anymore doesn't mean I can't give some fatherly advice."

"Daniel's fried chicken is better than yours, Billy," Carlos spat out before sitting beside Mark.

Billy nudged Hunter. "It really is. Do you think you can get me the recipe without him knowing it's for me?"

"I'll see what I can do. Okay, Carlos," Hunter turned his attention to him, "what's going on?"

Carlos looked down at the floor. "Nothing. It's nothing, really."

"Come on, you're with family now." Mark put a comforting arm around Carlos's shoulder.

Carlos's shoulder bumped Mark. "I know." Looking back up, he sighed. "Cameron and I have been fighting over Alex."

"Alex?" Hunter and Mark asked in unison.

Billy quickly clarified, "They are fighting because Carlos is being an idiot."

"I'm not being an idiot," Carlos argued. He paused for a moment, then added, "I'm worried Cameron is going to leave me for him."

Billy coughed the word, "Idiot."

"Billy," Hunter warned.

Mark squeezed Carlos's shoulder. "Why do you think he's going to leave you for Alex?"

"He and Alex have been talking a lot the past two weeks. Text. Emails. Phone calls," Carlos explained. "He says it's nothing I should worry about, but every time they talk, he leaves the room. What am I supposed to think? I'm pretty sure this special project he's doing is to visit Alex."

Mark asked, "Do you love him?"

"Yes," Carlos answered.

Mark then asked, "Do you trust him?

"Yes," Carlos answered. "But—"

Mark cut him off. "No, buts. Either you trust him or you don't. Do you trust him?"

"I trust him," Carlos replied shamefully. "It's that asshole Alex I don't trust."

Hunter jumped into the conversation. "It doesn't matter if you trust Alex or not. You trust Cameron. Doesn't he trust you to do this work and not do to him the same thing Alex did to him?"

"Yes," Carlos grumbled. "He does."

Crossing his arms, Billy added, "So what's the problem? You know he and Jordan are tighter than the shirts you wear. Nothing is going on. Jordan would tell me."

"You know!" Carlos accused.

Billy took a step back. "No! I don't! I don't even know what project he's working on now!"

"Liar!" Carlos jumped off the desk. "Jordan tells you everything! What's going on, Billy?"

Billy inched his way to the door. "I swear I don't know."

"Tell me," Carlos ordered, taking a step closer. "I have ways of making you talk."

107

Billy ran out of the room, yelling back, "I don't know!"

"Yes! You do!" Carlos shouted back, taking off after Billy.

Laughing, Hunter said, "Those two."

"We should stop them." Mark chuckled. "After I shower off." He picked his ruined shirt up off the ground. "Do you ever think about having kids?"

They heard Billy caterwauling with laughter in the other room. "Stop tickling me! I swear I don't know anything!"

"Then remember we have them?" Mark finished, shaking his head.

They heard Carlos ordering Billy, "Tell me!"

"Go get ready for the next shoot," Hunter said, laughing. "I'll break them up."

Mark pecked him on the cheek. "Don't ground them. They're supposed to take me out for my bachelor party tomorrow."

"I won't." Hunter pulled out his phone. "Why is Caleb calling me? He knows we're shooting."

Walking away, Mark commented, "Maybe he wants to film again. I'm off to shower." He stopped in the doorway and shouted, "Carlos! Don't put your dirty cock in his mouth! I have to kiss that mouth later!"

CHOCOLATE MOUSSE

"**HEY, ARE YOU** busy?" Paris asked, walking into the kitchen.

Daniel looked up from his phone. "I was about to start making a chocolate mousse for dessert tonight. Why? What's up?"

"I was lonely sitting in my office," Paris lied. "Would you mind if I came in here and worked off my phone while you cook?"

Daniel shrugged. "Sure. It's not really cooking. More mixing and piping."

"Sounds interesting. Distract me." Paris sat on a stool, then covertly opened his camera app and began recording. "Tell me how you make chocolate mousse."

Daniel pulled the mixing bowl out of the refrigerator. "Okay, well, first, we use a chilled bowl for mixing." He put it under the mixer. "Then we pour in heavy cream."

"How much?" Paris interrupted.

Pouring the cream into a measuring cup. "It's one cup per portion. I'm making ten portions. An extra two for Billy and Carlos. Hunter was right. They do eat a lot."

"They do," Paris commented, watching Daniel pour the heavy cream into the bowl. "Then what?"

Turning the mixer on, Daniel answered, "We whip until it thickens slightly and becomes frothy." Grabbing the cocoa powder, Daniel carefully measured out a cup. "While we wait, I'm going to sift one and a fourth cups of cocoa powder."

"Why do you do that?" Paris asked casually while he recorded Daniel sifting.

Tapping the sifter over the bowl, Daniel said, "It breaks apart the cocoa, so there's no dark spots in your mousse." Daniel peeked into the mixing bowl. "Looks like we're ready to mix in the cocoa and two cups of powdered sugar."

"Can you use regular sugar instead of powdered?" Paris asked, zooming in on Daniel pouring the cocoa into the mixing bowl.

Daniel carefully measured out a cup of powdered sugar. "No. You need powdered sugar, or the mousse will have a gritty feel to it when you eat it."

"Gritty?" Paris continued covertly recording as Daniel measured a second cup and added it to the mixing bowl. "Like eating sand?"

Daniel grabbed a rubber spatula and started scraping the sides of the bowl. "Yeah. Now you want to carefully mix this until you have stiff peaks." Setting the spatula aside, Daniel grabbed a small

brown bottle. "Now I add vanilla extract to mine. A teaspoon for this much."

"Can you use other extracts?" Paris prodded.

Watching the mousse thicken, Daniel responded, "Yeah, I've used strawberry, orange, and once I used root beer. You have to be careful with extracts because a little goes a long way and you don't want to overpower the dish with its flavor."

"Strawberries and chocolate." Paris zoomed in on Daniel's butt. "That sounds sexy."

Turning the mixer off, Daniel lifted the mixer and began scraping the blades with the spatula. "It was. I served it in chilled wine glasses with fresh sweet strawberries as garnish."

"That sounds heavenly." Paris moved the camera back up to record what Daniel was doing next. "How are you going to serve this mousse for everyone?"

Daniel pulled rocks glasses out of the cabinet above him. "I think I'm going to go simple with this one. When it's time to serve, I'm going to put one crème filled wafer stick in, a small swirl of fresh whipped cream, and dust it with more cocoa."

"Could you make one like that for me right now?" Paris asked while Daniel spooned the mousse into the glasses.

"No, it'll be ruined by the time dinner comes." Daniel turned his head, catching Paris recording him. "Are you recording me?"

Paris quickly stopped the recording and put his phone up. "No," he lied badly.

"Let me see your phone," Daniel ordered, setting aside the mousse.

III

Paris got up. "No."

"Paris," Daniel's voice was commanding, "why were you recording me?"

"I need to go to the bathroom," Paris said, dashing out of the kitchen.

Paris heard Daniel shout after him, "Paris!"

MEETING WITH THE PROFESSOR PART 2

AFTER FRESHLY SHOWERING, Mark was back behind the desk in a powder blue dress shirt, feeling more like a slutty professor than an actual professor. He still felt a little sore from Carlos's earlier fuck, but they were on a time crunch to get these scenes done before the weekend. He hoped Billy would be a bit gentler than Carlos.

"Excuse me, Professor Mark," Billy said innocently from the doorway. "Do you have a minute?"

Mark looked up from the fake document he was working on and smiled at Billy. "Of course I have time for one of my top students. Come on in. Have a seat."

"Thanks, I won't be long." Billy stepped in, shutting the door behind him. Sitting down, he said, "I wanted to talk to you about class. Specifically, how it has changed recently."

Shutting the laptop, Mark stood up and came around the desk. "What do you mean?" Mark leaned back against the desk. "I haven't changed anything with the class."

"Well, not the class itself." Billy ran his eyes over Mark's body. "I've tried to add to the class discussion, but lately, you've been ignoring my contribution while praising Carlos for his."

Mark crossed his arms over his chest. "You mean you've been trying to disrupt my class by trying to pick an intellectual fight with Carlos?"

"No," Billy protested. "He thinks he's the best. I just remind him that I am."

Mark massaged his temples with one hand. "Billy, I already talked to Carlos, and he's agreed to keep the peace in my class between you two. Can't you do the same?"

"What's in it for me?" Billy asked with a lopsided grin. He looked Mark up and down hungrily. "I mean, it would be asking a lot of me. How else would I show you that I'm your," Billy stood up and got close to Mark, "top student?

Mark swallowed uncomfortably. "Billy, I'm your professor. I, uh, could get into a lot of trouble..."

"I need to show you that I'm your top," Billy opened Mark's pants, "student somehow."

Mark let out a gasp when he felt Billy's hand move over his hard dick. "Billy!"

"Come on, Professor, if you're not going to let me enjoy my A in the class, at least let me enjoy your A in here." Billy finished the line with a sensual kiss.

This wasn't exactly the scene they'd intended to film. The words were what Dennis had written, but the execution was definitely not what he had envisioned. Hunter didn't seem to mind Billy's interpretation, and, truth be told, Mark was getting turned on. He definitely was going to enjoy seeing how this was going to turn out.

Billy grabbed the back of Mark's head. He pressed their foreheads together and said in a deep throaty voice, "When you see me in class, you're going to remember the taste of me on your lips and the feel of me in you, Professor."

"Oh, Billy," Mark moaned, kicking off his shoes.

The next moments were a blur for Mark. Billy, with his lithe yet muscular body, spun Mark around, pushed his pants down his thighs, and had Mark sitting in his black jockey shorts on the chair. Mark's pants were yanked off and sent flying. Billy's mouth found his while Billy made quick work of Mark's button-down.

"Billy, what are you doing?" Mark managed to gasp out when Billy pulled away slightly.

Billy's answer was a flick of his tongue on Mark's nose before he dropped down to his knees and buried his face in Mark's crotch. He mouthed Mark's dick through the cotton fibers. Mark ran a hand through Billy's short hair. He looked down to see Billy looking back up at him, grinning with the cloth-covered cock in his mouth. Mark knew he was in trouble now.

Billy licked his way up over Mark's hard six-pack, diverting to briefly circle Mark's nipples before moving up his neck and ending it with a kiss on

Mark's chin. He kissed Mark on the lips before slipping back down Mark's body. Mark raised his hips up, letting Billy slip the briefs down and off of Mark.

"Billy," Mark said as a warning when he saw the devilish glint in his eye.

Billy ignored the warning, lifting Mark's hard cock up and sucking on his balls. He was relentless in his teasing. Billy danced his tongue over Mark's smooth balls. First, the left, then the right, then back and forth before taking both in his mouth. Then he licked up to the tip, then flicked his tongue over the crown.

Mark gripped the chair and arched his hips up. Billy swallowed him down easily. Running his tongue along the underside of Mark's shaft, he drew out the pleasure by slowly sucking Mark. He slipped a hand under Mark, pushed a finger between Mark's tight cheeks, and gently stroked his pucker.

"Fuck, that feels good." Mark moaned, gripping the chair arms harder. "Suck me, Billy. Earn that top spot in my class."

Billy kept his pace slow and teasing. He edged Mark ever closer to his blasting point. He knew if he didn't do something soon, Billy would suck him to completion, and the scene would be ruined. They'd have to finish shooting later, and Mark knew he'd be completely spent after that.

He nudged Billy with his knee, and when that didn't work, he clenched his cheeks around Billy's finger. That got Billy's attention. He tugged his finger free from Mark's crushing clench and slowly pulled

off Mark's cock to the tip. He swirled his tongue over the crown before pulling off.

Trying to catch his breath and calm down, Mark watched Billy stand. In Mark's eyes, he moved in slow motion. First, he pulled his tight polo up and off. He kicked off his shoes before dropping his khaki shorts. He wasn't wearing underwear, allowing Mark to fully enjoy the view of his naked body.

It had been a long time since Mark had seen Billy naked in person. He'd seen some of his recent videos, but it was different right in front of your face. Billy now had a firm, hard chest that tapered down in a V shape to a trim, sculpted stomach. His cock jutting out from his hairless groin seemed bigger than before, almost rivaling Hunter's or Carlos's. Mark guessed it to be about eight inches.

"I've shown you what I can do, Professor." Billy's voice was seductive and alluring. He stroked his cock with his left hand. "Now, show me what you can do."

Mark pushed himself off the chair to land on his knees before Billy and his throbbing cock. He replaced Billy's hand with his. Looking up at the cocky young man, Mark said, "You're definitely going to need some extra attention in and out of class."

Mark wrapped his lips over the head of Billy's cock. He could taste Billy's pre-cum on his tongue. It was sweet, like honey. With his free hand, he fondled Billy's balls. Billy's legs trembled at the tender touch. Mark eased Billy's cock down, taking him easily into the back of his throat. He held himself there a moment before pulling back.

117

Mark continued caressing Billy's balls as he slowly suckled his cock. Moaning softly, Billy put a hand on Mark's shoulder to steady himself. Mark dragged his lips along Billy's shaft, making sure to run his tongue over the head to lap up Billy's delicious man juice. Teasing Billy was an added bonus.

Mark ignored the ache in his jaw. He and Billy were locked in a battle of who could tease the other the most. Mark was determined to win and have Hunter capture it all on camera. He knew he had won when he pressed his middle finger from the hand fondling Billy's balls in his taint.

"It's time I got that A." Billy pulled Mark up onto his feet.

Shrugging off his shirt, Mark turned around and kneeled on the chair. "It's yours for the taking."

"You bet it is." Billy ad-libbed with a playful smack. He leaned down and spat on Mark's hole. He rubbed it in with a finger. "This is the hottest ass on campus."

Billy's strong hands spread Mark's cheeks. Mark felt the first tentative swipe of Billy's tongue. The brush of Billy's tongue was gentle, yet tough. He swirled his tongue around, then did a zig-zag pattern, and finally started flicking his tongue into Mark.

"You're really earning that A," Mark moaned.

Billy squeezed Mark's toned ass. He started running his tongue up and down Mark's crack. He reached down under Mark with one hand and began stroking him. Mark let out a long, low groan. Billy released Mark's cock, licked up to the top of his crack, then stood up. Tapping his cock on Mark's ass.

Billy's voice was low and seductive when he spoke. "It's time for you to learn why I'll always be your top student."

Billy slowly pushed his cock into Mark's slick hole. Rolling his shoulders, Mark enjoyed the feel of Billy's hard cock sinking into him. With a hand on the small of Mark's back, Billy guided Mark to arch his back and stick his ass out. Billy's other hand was holding onto Mark's hip to steady him.

"Damn, that is a nice ass," Billy commented before he slowly started sawing his cock into Mark. Slapping Mark's ass, Billy asked, "Are you going to call on me more?"

Mark cried out, "Yes!"

"I didn't hear you." Billy smacked Mark's ass again.

Mark cried out again, "Yes!"

"You'd better, or you won't get this dick again." Billy grabbed Mark's other hip and began furiously pumping into Mark. "Yeah, you want this dick again, don't you, Professor?"

Mark growled deeply, "Every day."

After three more hard thrusts into Mark, Billy pulled out. He grabbed Mark by the hips, pulled him off the chair, and spun him around and back onto his desk. He lifted Mark's legs up, sending Mark onto his back. Billy plunged balls deep back into Mark. The sound of flesh slapping flesh sounded like an ovation from Billy's rapid thrusts.

Mark started stroking his cock. Billy was rubbing that special spot in him just right. When Billy's cock began to pulse in him, Mark felt tiny tremors of delight rushing through him. He was grateful that was a sign that Billy was almost done because he wasn't sure he could hold out much longer.

Billy pulled out and started jerking his cock. His breathing quickened. His face went into a quiet snarl. He thrust his hips forward, covering Mark's hole and balls in his creamy white juices. This set Mark off, and he began coating his stomach and chest with wild jerks.

Billy ran a hand through the fluids on Mark's stomach. "I'll see you after class."

DO YOU THINK THEY'D NOTICE
IF I MADE POPCORN?

"**H**OME SWEET HOME.**" Mark shut the door behind him. "I'm glad Billy and Carlos decided to stay and help clean up. We'll get a little normalcy."

"No!" they heard Daniel yell. "I'm not doing it!"

Then came Paris's plea, "Come on. Take it out for me. I need it."

"So much for normalcy," Hunter groaned.

They heard Paris continue, "Just take it out for me. I'll do all the work."

"What the Hell?" Mark asked, looking at Hunter in confusion.

They heard Paris add, "If we hurry, we can do it before everyone gets back."

"I can't believe you!" Daniel yelled back. "I told you I didn't want to do it!"

Paris then asked, "What if we did it at my place tonight? We can do the whole thing all over again."

Hunter asked Mark, "I thought they weren't fucking."

"I have a really nice spatula you can use," Paris continued.

Mark's eyes went wide. "Did he just say spatula?"

"Please, Daniel," they heard Paris beg. "I'm down on my knees."

Hunter rushed forward. "I'm putting a stop to this." Hunter busted into the kitchen. "What the Hell is going on in here?"

Following Hunter in, Mark said, "I thought you said you two weren't…" he paused when he saw the bewilderment on the two young men's faces, "fucking."

"We're not," Paris responded, baffled.

Crossing his arms, Hunter gave them a disapproving, fatherly glare. "We heard you."

"Yeah!" Mark added. Then slyly said with a hint of pride in his voice, "A spatula? I knew you were a secret freak."

Daniel and Paris looked at each other in confusion, then opened their eyes wide at the realization of what was overheard. Together they said, "No! No! No!"

"You can have my 'Daddy's Bitch' shirt," Mark said with a wink.

Gawking, Paris exclaimed, "I'm not his bitch!"

"I sort of am his daddy, though," Daniel commented.

Outraged, Paris turned to Daniel. "You are not my daddy!"

"You called me daddy earlier!" Daniel reminded him.

Flustered, Paris countered with, "Well, I held you while you slept last night!"

"So? I like being the little spoon!" Daniel shot back. "I've been solving your problems all week!"

Nudging Hunter, Mark whispered, "What are we watching?"

"I'm not sure," Hunter whispered back. "Do you think they'd notice if I made popcorn?"

"Lexi solved the problem with the officiant!" Paris barked back.

They both fell silent when Mark yelled, "What?!"

"The guy I hired backed out this morning," Paris answered timidly.

Daniel jumped to his rescue. "He already has a replacement." He nudged Paris.

"Ryan from Walden Woods is going to officiate," Paris clarified. "See? Everything is handled."

Mark narrowed his eyes at the two. "Is it? What were you two fighting about?"

"Hold up." Hunter pulled out his phone. "I want to hear this, too." Putting the phone to his ear, he said, "What do you got for me, Caleb? Uh-huh. They're sure? Okay. Thanks for telling me. Goodbye."

Mark looked at Hunter expectantly. When he didn't say anything, Mark said, "Well? What was that about?"

"Michael, the one that died, they think it was murder," Hunter said solemnly.

Shocked, Daniel said, "I thought he died of a heart attack."

"They were suspicious since he didn't have a history of heart problems and was a marathon runner."

123

Hunter put an arm around Mark. "The coroner is a big reader, and on a whim, they tested for digoxin." At the confused looks, Hunter continued, "It's a popular poison in books and movies. They found traces of it in his blood and in his coffee cup."

After a brief silence, Mark asked, "Daddy Twink?"

"Why is everything Daddy Twink's fault?" Daniel spat out bitterly.

Hunter cut off the argument. "We don't know it's Daddy Twink, but all these strange occurrences started happening when we got that flash drive from him. Paris, have you been able to schedule that meeting with him?"

"No, he turned off his messages. Let me see if he turned them back on." Paris began scrolling through his phone. "Oh, shit."

"What?" Daniel looked at his phone. "What the fuck?"

"What's going on?" Mark pulled out his own phone and looked up Daddy Twink's account. "Is this asshole blasting us on social media because we won't give him an audition?"

Hunter took Mark's phone. "Let me see that." Reading the screen, he said, "That little shit."

"Someone must have hacked his account," Daniel suggested.

Hunter handed Mark back his phone. "Paris, pull his account up on the computer so we can look together. We're going to need you to subscribe to his fan content so we can get some more information."

"He, um, gave me a free year after I messaged him last time," Paris said timidly before heading to his office.

"He wears that hood in all of his videos." Everyone trailed behind Paris to his desk and watched him pull up Daddy Twink's account. "I've been through all his videos, twice. There's nothing other than that mole on his dick I could use to identify him with."

Mark put a hand on Paris's shoulder and leaned into the screen. "Hunter, look at this guy Daddy Twink is fucking. He's wearing a diamond mask, but is it?"

"It is." Hunter took the mouse from Paris and paused the video on the screen. "That bastard. I need to call Caleb."

Turning his head from Mark to Hunter, Paris asked, "What is it?"

"That's the punk that almost hit me with his car," Mark answered.

Hunter straightened. "I'm going to call Caleb. We need to find out who this Daddy Twink guy is."

THE ELEPHANT IN THE ROOM

"**T**HANKS FOR LETTING me crash here tonight." Daniel plopped down on Paris's couch. "I really don't want to see my roommates right now."

Handing Daniel a water, Paris sat down. "What was the fight over?"

"They went onto my computer and did some stuff that they knew they shouldn't have done," Daniel answered vaguely. "I'll sleep on the couch. I have to get up early and stop by my place to get a change of clothes."

Paris scoffed. "You slept in my bed last night. You can sleep in it tonight." Paris winked at him. "You can be the little spoon."

"Thanks. I still have to go get some clothes in the morning." Daniel laughed.

Paris shrugged. "You can wear some of mine. We're about the same size."

"In most places." Daniel subconsciously grabbed himself. "I'm not fitting into your cute bikini briefs."

Paris made a disbelieving face. "I've seen your ass. It's not bigger than mine. Better maybe, but not bigger."

"I'm not talking about my ass." Daniel winked at him again. "I was blessed or cursed, depending on how you see it."

Paris joked, "I haven't seen it." He patted Daniel's knee. "Look at me solving all your problems. Call me Daddy Paris."

"No," Daniel said firmly. "I'm the daddy; you're the boy."

Paris felt a stir in his pants at being called his boy. "Anyway, do you think we should tell Mark and Hunter that you're the one cooking for the reception?"

"Depends. Do you think Mark will freak out and blame Daddy Twink for it?" Daniel asked bitterly.

Taken aback, Paris responded, "Hey, he has a right to be suspicious after that note and that mean tweet."

"He deleted the tweet." Daniel muttered something under his breath that Paris didn't hear. "You don't think it's Daddy Twink, do you?"

Paris thought for a moment. "I don't know. It could be, but I want to believe that it's all a coincidence. How could he know Mark's schedule for that muscled boy to almost hit him, or know who was catering the wedding? That asshole canceling officiating on us is totally not on him."

"It's not him," Daniel said fervently.

Paris put his hands up in placation. "Okay. Okay."

"Sorry, I'm just on edge after today." Daniel took a swig of water. "I didn't mean to take it out on you."

Paris grinned slyly. "Maybe cooking something will help relax you?"

"Maybe." Daniel took another drink, then realized what Paris was trying to do. "You asshole. I'm not doing a cooking show for you."

Paris made his voice as sweet as possible. "But Daddy."

"No. Keep it up, and I'll put you over my knee." Daniel laughed.

Paris purred out, "Oh, Daddy."

Daniel nearly spit out the water he was drinking. "You brat." He tapped Paris on the arm. "Do you mind if I grab a shower?"

"Make yourself at home." Paris got up. "I'll find you something you can wear."

Following Paris, Daniel suspiciously asked, "It's not a 'Daddy's Bitch' shirt, is it?"

"No." Paris laughed. "Come on, I'll grab you some fresh towels."

Paris sat on the couch, waiting with eager anticipation for Daniel to finish showering. He decided to be funny and leave Daniel the novelty underwear he had bought on a whim, but wasn't bold enough to wear even in private. He didn't know why he still had them, but he was glad he did.

Paris stifled a laugh when he heard Daniel yell, "Paris! Are you serious?"

"What do you mean?!" Paris called back, trying to sound innocent. Hearing Daniel's footsteps coming closer, he tried to control his laughter.

Daniel appeared, wearing a towel and a scowl. "You think you're funny, don't you?"

"What do you mean?" Paris asked, giggling.

Daniel unwrapped his towel, revealing the novelty underwear. "This." Paris was speechless, seeing an elephant face plastered on Daniel's groin. The ears stuck out along Daniel's narrow hips, and the overstuffed trunk dangled down almost to his knee. "Come find me something I can really wear, please."

"I, um, I," Paris stuttered out. His jaw dropped when Daniel turned around, giving Paris an uncensored view of his firm cheeks with a thin sting separating them. "Damn."

When he got to the bedroom, Daniel had the towel back on. "Asshole." He tossed the elephant undies at Paris. "I should make you wear them."

"Not after you stretched them out." Paris swallowed hard. "Damn. I think you're bigger than Daddy Twink."

Daniel groaned. "Is he all you think about?"

"No. No." Paris went to his dresser and rummaged through his underwear drawer. "When you said you were blessed, I didn't think you meant blessed with a capital B." Paris found an old pair of lime green trunks. Tossing them to Daniel, he said, "These might work."

Daniel slipped them on under his towel. "Thank you."

"I didn't mean to embarrass you." Paris found some gym shorts and a tee.

Daniel hit Paris in the face with the towel. "You didn't." He took the clothes from Paris. "I'm a go-go boy, remember? I wear that type of stuff all the time. Even skimpier."

"Really?" Paris choked out.

Pulling the shirt on, he said, "Yeah. I'll go make us something to eat while you shower."

"Okay," Paris said, trying to picture Daniel wearing less.

Daniel tweaked Paris's nose. "Don't be long, and no recording me secretly."

In the shower, Paris couldn't get the image of Daniel in the elephant underwear out of his head. *That trunk was halfway down his leg.* Paris soaped himself, careful not to touch his own growing cock. *He wasn't even hard.* Rinsing off, he turned the hot water off, hoping the cold would shock away his excitement.

He's your friend, Paris told himself as he dried off. *You don't have many of those, so don't fuck it up.* Stepping back into his bedroom, he saw the elephant underwear lying on the floor. Picking them up, he debated. *It'll make him laugh, at least.*

Mustering all his courage, Paris stepped out into the living room. Daniel was busy with his back to him at the stove. Paris crossed his arms over his chest, then uncrossed them. He thought about turning around and leaving before Daniel saw him. Daniel chose that moment to turn around.

"What are you wearing?" Daniel asked, laughing.

Paris bounced from one foot to the other. "I felt bad about leaving you these, so..." Paris's words

trailed off. "I know it was stupid and inappropriate. Let me go and change."

"Don't you dare." Daniel turned off the stove, then came around into the living room. "Look at you being all bold and sexy."

Paris felt a mix of pride and embarrassment. "I don't look as good as you in them." Paris placated.

"You look sexy as hell." Daniel took Paris's hand and made him twirl. "Look at those cakes!" Daniel smacked his ass. "If this job with Hunter and Mark doesn't work out, I think I can get you a job dancing on the bar. How's your dancing?"

Blushing, Paris said, "Horrible."

"I doubt that." Daniel pulled out his phone and started playing dance music. "Come on, show me what you got."

Bashful, Paris said, "I don't know how to dance."

"Come on, if you can have sex, you can dance." Daniel spun him around again so Paris's bare ass was against him. Putting his hands on Paris's bare hips, Daniel said, "Relax and follow my movements."

Paris felt Daniel's crotch rub against his bare ass. "Um, ok."

"Feel the beat and go with it," Daniel instructed. "Like that, perfect."

Moving his hips, Paris began to sway along with Daniel. "You know I could do this with more clothes on."

"Where's the fun in that?" Daniel whispered in his ear.

Paris swallowed hard, trying to find his voice. He finally managed to eke out, "Aren't you supposed to be cooking?"

"And ignore the elephant in the room?" Daniel moved his hands from Paris's hips to join in front of his stomach. "You're a good guy, Paris, you know that? One day I hope to find a good guy like you." Daniel abruptly let go and moved away. "Go put on some pants. You're not eating my food dressed like that."

Paris couldn't turn around for fear of Daniel seeing the trunk of the elephant standing up. "I should change out of these."

"I didn't say that." Daniel gave Paris's ass a playful squeeze. "But don't go to bed wearing that. It's not comfortable."

Paris had a million questions for Daniel; instead he responded, "Oh, okay."

PILLOW TALK

LYING IN BED with his head on Hunter's chest, Mark asked, "Did Caleb get back to you on the Todd thing?"

"Todd never saw Daddy Twink's face. Never heard him speak, either," Hunter answered, rubbing Mark's back. "A mutual friend of theirs set it up months ago. He said he forgot the video even existed and asked if we could get it taken down."

Mark played with the hairs on Hunter's chest. "Have you told Dennis what's going on?"

"No." Hunter let out a deep breath. "There's really nothing to tell him. Nothing really ties Daddy Twink to everything except coincidence."

Sitting up in the bed, Mark looked Hunter in the face. "Why is this all happening now of all times? All I want to do is to marry you."

"You will." Hunter pulled Mark into his arms. "Paris is on top of it."

Mark mumbled into Hunter's chest, "And Daniel is on top of Paris, apparently."

"Not yet, but I don't doubt he will be soon." Hunter's chest shook with laughter. "I've been wondering when he was going to finally work up the nerve to speak to Paris."

Mark pulled away from Hunter to look at him. "Wait. What?"

"Come on, you haven't noticed it?" Hunter brushed the hair along Mark's head. "For the last three months, he's been finding every excuse to talk to Paris, and Paris has been too oblivious to notice." Hunter did his best impression of Daniel. "'Paris, I'm done unless you have anything else you'd like me to do.' 'Paris, do you want me to clean under your desk?' 'Paris, I'm going to vacuum the bedrooms now; let me know if it disturbs you.'"

Mark dropped his head back into Hunter's chest. "Oh, my God. That's like when you were trying to flirt with me when we first met." Mark deepened his voice to sound like Hunter. "'Mark, do you want to go over the lines again?' 'Mark, let me know if I hurt you.' 'Mark, do you need me to use more lube?' 'Mark, here's a water in case you get thirsty.'"

"I was not that bad," Hunter argued. Then amended, "Okay, I was. You didn't make it easy."

Looking back at Hunter, Mark said, "I had no clue. It wasn't until Dennis asked me to go to lunch with you guys and then didn't show."

"He got tired of me pining after you." Hunter laughed. "I didn't know you were coming to lunch, and when you sat down, I was scared shitless."

134

Mark tweaked Hunter's nipple. "The big dick Hunter Adams, the Destroyer of Holes, was scared of me."

"Everyone wanted to film with you, and I was a nobody then. You were at the bottom of the hour, remember? I was trying to make a name for myself; you already had one." Hunter pulled Mark's head down to kiss him on the forehead. "Now you're my bottom."

Smiling down at Hunter, Mark said, "Forever and always."

"I can't wait to plunge my dick back into you after tomorrow's shoot," Hunter growled.

Mark patted his chest. "Well, if those boys do to me what they did today, you may have to wait another day."

"I shouldn't have told them to see who could tease you more," Hunter groaned.

Mark smacked Hunter's chest. "You bastard!" He kissed Hunter on the lips. "They did a good job, but I think turnabout is fair play."

"What do you mean?" Hunter asked, worried.

Coyly, Mark said, "I think it's time they got a taste of their own medicine."

"Mark," Hunter rolled them over so he was on top of him, "what are you going to do?"

Mark danced his fingers down Hunter's sides. "Maybe pit the boys against each other and see who wins. It'll make for a hot video."

"I like that idea." Hunter ground his crotch into Mark. "I'll talk to Billy. You get Carlos."

Licking his lips, Mark said, "Then I can get you."

"We're bad parents, aren't we?" Hunter continued rubbing his groin against Mark's.

With a hint of devilishness, Mark said, "Yes, but we're good at being bad."

THE CLICK OF A BUTTON

PARIS SAVED THE email he'd written an hour ago back to his drafts. It was hard to believe that his future rested on the click of a button. Once he hit send, it was out there in cyberspace going to Mark, Hunter, Dennis, and Lexi Luscious. That's why he had to be sure; there was no taking it back once he hit send.

"Why have you been so quiet?" Daniel's question startled Paris out of his thoughts. "Do you have another migraine?"

Paris shook his head. "No, no. I'm just trying to decide whether or not to do something risky."

"How risky?" Daniel asked with concern, spinning Paris's chair to face him.

Paris looked into Daniel's concerned face. He wanted to tell him everything but didn't want to chance Daniel getting mad. He settled on being as vague as possible. "They'll either praise me or fire me."

"Do you really think they'd fire you?" Daniel asked, crouching down to look into his eyes.

Paris thought for a moment. "No."

"Do you, in your heart of hearts, believe it's a good idea?" Daniel asked.

Paris bit his lower lip before cautiously answering, "I do, but it'll make someone mad."

"Will they get over it?" Daniel questioned.

A knot formed in the pit of Paris's stomach. "God, I hope so."

"As long as it's coming from a good place, I'm sure they will," Daniel reassured him. "Sometimes it's better to ask forgiveness than permission."

Paris nodded. "Okay." He looked at Daniel pointedly. "Could the same thing be said about what your roommates did? Did what they do come from a good place?"

"No." Daniel stood. "What they did was wrong, and they know it." He took in a deep breath and exhaled loudly. "I do need to talk to them. I can't ignore them all night while dancing on the bar next to them."

Paris reached out and took Daniel's hand. "Did they at least mean well?"

Daniel rolled his eyes. "Yes."

"What did they do?" Paris prodded.

Daniel squeezed his hand. "I don't want to talk about it, but they did complicate some things."

"Alright, change of subject," Paris announced. "The reception. How do you feel about cooking for 25 people?"

Daniel shook his head. "Another reason I need to make up with my roommates. I need them to help prepare and serve."

"You do have this, right?" Paris tried to keep the panic out of his voice. "Please, tell me you got this."

Daniel flashed him a confident smile. "I do. Michael gave me the keys to the shop. I actually have to leave in a little bit to meet the food delivery."

"Do you want me to go with you?" Paris hoped Daniel would say yes to ease his fears.

"No, but you could come out tonight and support me." Daniel winked at him. "I'll come by your place and make us dinner before we go to the bar."

Paris's mouth went dry at the thought of seeing Daniel in skimpy underwear. "Um, how—" Paris cleared his throat to keep his voice from squeaking. "How am I going to support you? Put money in your, um," Paris cleared his throat again, "put money in your underwear?"

"You can if you want, but really, I need someone to go in the back with me to help me change outfits and hold my money for me." Daniel blushed a little. "You're going to see more of me and others than you probably would like."

Paris gave Daniel an incredulous look. "There's a sex jar in the kitchen for every time I catch Hunter and Mark having sex."

"Is that what that is?" Daniel busted out laughing. "I've wanted to ask about that since I started, but I was scared of the answer!"

Paris shook his head. "We donate the money to charity at the end of the month." He closed his eyes and shook his head. "We donate about a thousand dollars a month."

"Damn," Daniel said, wide-eyed. "I want to love someone that much that I can't keep my hands off them."

Paris sighed. "Me too."

"Okay, I need to get going if I'm going to meet the delivery." Daniel took a step away. "Text me when you get home, and I'll come over and cook for you."

Paris pulled out his keys and took one off the ring. "Take my spare key in case I run late."

"Are you sure?" Daniel asked, taking the key.

Without hesitation, Paris said, "Yeah. You're trusting me with your money tonight; I think I can trust you with my key."

"Okay." Daniel popped the key onto his ring. "I'll see you when you get home."

"See you when I get home." Paris smiled, watching Daniel leave.

He turned back to his computer. Paris opened the email back up. He mulled over Daniel's words from earlier. *In my heart of hearts, I know this is the right thing to do.* He hovered the mouse over the send button. *He'll be mad at first, but I know he'll forgive me.* Paris clicked send. *It's sometimes better to ask forgiveness than permission. At least, I hope so.* The email with the unedited video of Daniel cooking flew off into cyberspace.

140

MEETING WITH THE
PROFESSOR PART 3

"**WHAT ARE YOU** doing here?" Billy asked with contempt when he entered the office and saw Carlos sitting there.

Jumping up from his seat, Carlos returned the disdain. "I have a meeting with Professor Mark. What are you doing here?"

"You are obviously as mistaken as you are about those cargo shorts still being in style," Billy quipped. "Now, please, leave. Professor Mark and I have important things we need to discuss."

Eyeing Billy up and down, Carlos responded, "You really need to see someone about your delusions of grandeur."

"Look at you using big words!" Billy exclaimed cattily. "Do you even know what they mean?"

Carlos stepped forward so he and Billy were chest to chest. "Do you, simpleton?"

"Boys!" Mark exclaimed, walking in. "What's going on in here?"

Billy kept his eyes locked with Carlos's when he said, "I was just about to ask the janitor to take this trash out for you."

"I think we should call for medical help." Carlos gave Billy a sneer. "It's obvious he's had a head trauma and thinks he's clever."

Shutting the door behind him, Mark put a hand on each of the boys' shoulders. "I asked you both here because I want you to play nicely with each other," Mark gave their shoulders a squeeze, "and me."

"What?" they said in unison, turning their attention to Mark.

Angry, Carlos asked, "Are you fucking him?"

"He's fucking us both," Billy answered.

"Actually, you two are fucking me." Mark smiled devilishly. "I brought us here together so we can come," Mark made his voice sultry, "together."

"How hard has your head been hitting the headboard?" Billy asked.

Carlos chimed in, "Obviously too hard if he thinks this is going to happen."

"Carlos is the one that taught me…" Billy's eyes grew big when Mark pretended to whisper in his ear. "Billy's the one that showed me how to…" Carlos's eyes did the same when Mark pretended to whisper in his ear. "What do you say, boys?"

Billy cleared his throat. "I don't think I really gave Carlos a fair chance."

"I think there might be some benefit to this." Carlos eyed Billy salaciously.

Moving his hands to the back of their heads, Mark said, "Good, now let's seal the deal with a kiss." Mark brought their faces together to kiss. "So hot," he moaned, watching the boys kiss.

Guiding their heads to his, Mark joined the kiss. Tongues slipped in and out of mouths, dancing and twisting with each other. Mark's hands moved down the boys' backs to rest on their youthful asses. He felt Billy take a caressing hold of his left cheek, Carlos a firm hold on the right.

Pulling back, Mark pulled Billy's shirt up and off. With Billy's chest exposed, Carlos immediately pounced onto Billy's left nipple, leaving Mark the right to tease. He steadied Billy with a hand on his back, while his other was groping Billy's hard cock through his pants.

Mark heard Billy moaning, low and deep. Lowering Billy's zipper, Mark pulled his cock and balls out. He gave Billy a few tender strokes before letting go to push Carlos down to the jutting cock. Mark guided Carlos back and forth along Billy's prick while he moved up to kiss Billy's moaning mouth.

Billy had one hand on Carlos's shoulder, the other held onto Mark tightly. Mark pulled away from the kiss. He slipped down Billy's body, nudging Carlos aside. On their knees, with Billy's hard cock between them, they ran their mouths along Billy's shaft. At first, they moved in opposite directions, but soon Mark and Carlos synced up.

With a hand on each of their shoulders, Billy began thrusting his hips through their lips. Mark dipped down to suck on Billy's balls, while Carlos

resumed deep-throating Billy. After a few minutes, Carlos and Mark wordlessly swapped places, letting Mark tease Billy with the swipe of his tongue over his crown.

When Mark felt Billy's legs tremble, he knew it was time to change partners. Releasing Billy from his mouth, Mark stood, taking Carlos up along with him. Pulling off Carlos's shirt, Mark guided him back against the desk. Billy was already on his knees, undoing Carlos's pants and pulling out his cock.

With Billy swallowing down Carlos's cock, Mark worked Carlos's nipples, rubbing one with his fingers while flicking his tongue over the other. He heard Carlos letting out deep, guttural groans. With both hands rubbing Carlos's nipples, Mark moved to muffle Carlos's groans with a kiss.

"It's nice to see you two getting along." Mark took a step back and began unbuttoning his shirt. Kicking off his shoes, he dropped his pants and said, "How about some teacher appreciation?"

Standing up, Billy said in a deep husky voice, "Gladly."

"You are our favorite professor, after all," Carlos said, his words dripping with lust.

Mark stretched out his arms. Billy went to the left, Carlos to the right. He kissed Billy first, then Carlos. Billy dropped down, while Carlos slipped around Mark. Billy's warm mouth engulfed Mark's dick while Carlos's tongue flittered between Mark's spread cheeks. Mark's legs quivered from the pleasure onslaught.

"You two work so well together," Mark moaned, reaching around to pull Carlos into his ass while using the other hand to pull Billy onto his cock. "I foresee a lot of group projects in our future."

Carlos licked his way back up along Mark's spine until he was on his feet. He growled in Mark's ear, "I hope there will be some deep penetrating discussions." Carlos angled his cock into Mark and pushed in.

"Yes!" Mark yelled, nearly choking Billy when he thrust his hips forward.

Billy then licked his way up along Mark's stomach, over his chest, and along the length of his neck. "I'm ready for my oral examination." Billy bent Mark down to bob on his cock.

Spit roasted by the two boys, Mark bounced back and forth, taking Carlos's ten inches easily while swallowing Billy's eight inches. After some time, the two boys swapped places. When his legs began to ache, Mark went to his knees. Billy followed, never letting his cock slip from Mark's ass.

Mark pulled off Carlos's cock. With a hand wrapped around the base, he offered it to Billy behind him. Forcing Mark onto all fours, Billy didn't lose any of his momentum, humping into Mark while he hungrily devoured Carlos's cock. Mark managed to take Carlos's cock back for a few moments before they shifted again.

The two boys pulled out almost simultaneously. Mark flipped onto his back. Carlos had Mark's legs pressed to his chest. Billy had his cock dangling by Mark's head. Carlos pressed himself in. When he

groaned, Billy quieted him by shoving his cock into Mark's mouth, then began humping his face.

"I hope we get extra credit for this," Carlos said, pistoning his cock in and out of Mark.

Pulling his cock out of Mark's mouth, Billy moved behind Carlos. "I think you need some help." Billy pushed his cock into Carlos's tight ass.

"Fuck!" Carlos shouted, ping-ponging himself between Billy and Mark.

It was only minutes before Carlos sat up and pulled his cock of Mark to jerk his load out. Billy had a hand on his shoulder and another on Carlos's hip. He didn't stop fucking Carlos, not even when the white streams of his seed flew from his cock to coat Mark. When Carlos shook, Billy finally pulled out.

Carlos fell to the side and moved to lie next to Mark. Billy was between Mark's legs, jerking his cock as Mark was pulling on his. Mark arched his hips up and made grunting sounds when his orgasm hit, splatting himself with his post-coitus juices. Billy's shuddering climax followed just a moment later, speckling the few remaining empty patches of Mark's skin.

Moving to lie on Mark's other side, Billy panted, "Don't you need a TA for next semester?"

"Maybe two?" Carlos asked.

Laughing with delight, Mark answered, "I'll see what I can do."

25

YOU CAN FUCK ANY OF THE BOYS EXCEPT PARIS

"I **DID NOT TELL** Billy to stick his penis in you!" Mark shouted at Carlos before stepping into the office. He grinned at Hunter, who was sitting behind the desk, looking at his phone. "He came up with that one all on his own."

From behind him, he heard Billy shout, "We're heading back with Brad and Cody! See you at the house!"

"If I wasn't so spent from today, I'd say we test the weight limit of this desk again," Mark joked. He crossed his arms when he got no response from Hunter. "Hunter." Mark moved around the desk and put his hand over the phone. "Hunter!"

Startled, Hunter pulled out his earbuds. "I'm sorry. I was watching the video Paris sent of Daniel cooking. Did you watch it yet?"

"No, you have my phone." Mark looked at the screen. "What video?"

Hunter sat his phone down. "Paris recorded Daniel making chocolate mousse yesterday without him knowing."

"That's what they were fighting about when we came in!" Mark exclaimed, snapping his fingers.

Hunter turned in his chair and pulled Mark down into his lap. "Anyway, the video is only what Paris could sneak on his phone. Paris said it was a rough idea of the cooking show we should do."

"I take it from how you were engrossed in your phone that it was a good video." Mark put his arms around Hunter's neck. "Do you think Lexi will like it?"

Hunter hugged Mark close. "She already texted me and Dennis that she wants to do it."

"Why do you look worried, then?" Mark asked.

Hunter's breath heaved with the deep breath he took. "The way she wants to do it may not make everyone happy."

"You can't make everyone happy." Mark snuggled into him. "We need to get going soon if we're going to make our reservations."

Hunter teased, "I'm not the one that takes forever to get ready."

"Excuse me?" Mark tried to pull away, but Hunter held him close. "I wouldn't take so long if you didn't keep putting your dick in me."

Hunter playfully chided, "To be fair, you're always bending over to pick up the soap."

"What's wrong with that?" Mark asked innocently.

Nuzzling Mark's chest, Hunter growled out, "We use liquid body wash."

"Well, there's that." Mark laughed. "Too bad we won't get to play before dinner."

Hunter griped, "At least you've had orgasms."

"I give you permission to fuck any of the boys tonight," Mark announced. Then thought about it, "Except Paris. You might break him."

Cheekily, Hunter said, "But he has a brand new spatula."

"The images I got when I heard him say that." Mark chuckled. "I'm getting him a 'Daddy's Bitch' shirt."

Hunter grinned at Mark. "I got him a shirt, but it doesn't say that exactly."

"What does it say?" Mark asked.

Pushing Mark off his lap, Hunter stood. "You'll see when we get to the house. You can watch the video in the car."

"We brought your truck," Mark corrected. "We're not going through that again."

DANIEL IS GOING TO KICK MY ASS

PARIS JUMPED WHEN he heard Dennis shout, "Is anyone home?!"

"I'm in the office!" Paris shouted back. Heading into the foyer, he nearly collided with Dennis. "Dennis, I'm so sorry."

Dennis pulled the young man into an enthusiastic hug. "Hey! It's so good to see you!"

"It's good to see you, too." Paris hugged him back. "Where's Benjamin?"

Letting go of Paris, Dennis took Paris by the hand and pulled him into the living room. "He's getting the luggage. I want to hear about that sexy twink in the video you sent."

"You mean Daniel?" Paris asked, letting himself be pulled down onto the couch. "He's the cleaning guy that took on the cooking duties this week. "

Dennis leaned back into the couch and said, "What's his stage name? When can I shoot with him?"

"He doesn't have a stage name. He's not a performer." Paris paused. "Wait, did you just say you wanted to shoot with him? Are you going to start filming again?"

Dennis gave Paris a coy smile. "Benjamin and I have been talking, and we decided I should make a limited comeback."

"Hunter said he was all against dating someone who worked in the adult film industry. What changed his mind?" Paris asked curiously.

"He got to see the work." Dennis shrugged. "Like most people, he thought that you showed up, said your lines, then went at it. Now he knows it's hours of getting the lighting right, getting aroused, faking moans and groans, then blowing your load on command."

Paris nodded. "Those shoots can be long."

"He also saw I wasn't happy not being in front of the camera." Dennis playfully tapped Paris on the arm. "Are you sure he doesn't want to film? I know you two have to get your cooking show in order, but if he's interested, I can work with your schedule."

Paris did a double take. "Wait. Film our cooking show? What cooking show?"

"Didn't Lexi email you?" Dennis grimaced when Paris shook his head. "Shit. She texted me and Hunter. I figured she sent you an email or something."

Paris asked sternly, "Dennis, spit it out."

"She wants Daniel to be a sexy cook," he paused to grin at Paris, "for you while you ask questions."

"Dennis! If you don't come help me with this luggage, I'm going to throw away all your jocks!" Benjamin yelled from the front door.

Dennis grabbed Paris's hand and gave it a squeeze. "He won't throw them away. He likes the way I look in them." He winced when he heard crashing coming from the door. "I better go help him. I can't wait to see the show, and if he changes his mind about performing, let me know."

"Daniel's going to kick my ass," Paris said to himself in shock.

THE HOTTEST MAN WITH
THE HOTTEST ASS

"**IT'S NOT FAIR,**" Mark grumbled as he pulled on the tight black tee with "Sperm Bank" emblazoned in bright white across the front. "How did I end up with Billy and Carlos taking me out for my bachelor party, and you got Dennis and Benjamin?"

"I have no idea." Hunter pointed to the words on Mark's shirt. "You are putting something over that for dinner, right?"

Mark pulled on a white dress shirt. "Of course." Buttoning the shirt up only enough to cover the words, Mark asked, "Can I at least get Brad or Cody to come with us since Jordan and Cameron are delayed?"

"That's up to them." Hunter picked a stray thread off Mark's shirt. "Did they tell you what they were planning?"

Mark pulled on his ball-hugging jeans. "No, and they giggle evilly every time I ask. What is Dennis doing for you?"

"He didn't say, and I didn't ask." Hunter pulled on a pair of khaki pants. He grinned smugly at Mark when he said, "I trust him and didn't pit him sexually against his best friend."

Mark ruffled Hunter's hair. "Asshole. You planned this."

"I did not!" Hunter stepped away from Mark. "Watch the hair; it took me five minutes to get it right."

Mark shook his head in disbelief. "Tell me again why I'm marrying you?"

"Because no one can wreck your walls the way I can," Hunter said with a smug grin before tugging on his blue button-down. "That and I don't complain that it takes you 45 minutes to gel, mousse, style, tease, spritz, and whatever else you do to your hair."

Mark came over and started buttoning his shirt for him. "And why don't you complain?"

"Because I like to tell everyone the hottest man with the hottest ass in the room is my man." Hunter gave him a gentle kiss.

Mark gave him a smug grin. "Don't you ever forget it."

"Too bad Paris has plans tonight. He could have been your emotional support twink," Hunter said, pulling away to tuck in his shirt.

Grabbing his shoes, Mark sat on the bed to put them on. "I'd rather have Daniel. What did they call him?" He thought for a second. "An attack twink"

"When twinks attack." Hunter laughed. "That sounds like a gay horror movie."

Mark chuckled. "Or a Tuesday here."

Hunter sat on the bed to slip on his own shoes. "I wonder if Paris is ever going to wear the shirt I got him."

"He'll probably wear it every chance he gets." Mark stood up. "Shall we go?"

LOTION ME UP?

PARIS FROZE IN shock when he walked through his apartment door. He counted four coolers stacked two high in his apartment. "Daniel?" he called out, shutting the door behind him. "What's going on?"

Daniel popped from around the corner, talking on his phone. He held a finger up to Paris. "You can? Great. I'll be over in a little bit. You're a lifesaver." Daniel nodded his head. "Yes, this makes up for what you guys did. I'll see you soon." Daniel hung up his phone. "Catastrophe averted."

"What catastrophe? Why is my apartment filled with coolers?" Paris asked, a little dumbfounded.

Daniel came over and took Paris by the hand. "Why don't we sit on the couch?"

"Daniel, what's going on?" Paris asked, letting himself be led to the couch. "You're scaring me."

Sitting down with Paris, Daniel said, "Don't freak out. I've got it all covered."

"If you don't spit it out," Paris warned.

Daniel patted his hand. "When I went to take delivery of the food, the police had the M and M Catering office taped off. They still aren't letting anyone in."

"All these coolers?" Paris looked over at the coolers.

"Have the food for the wedding," Daniel finished. "The driver didn't want to have to take it all back and unload it, so he gave me the coolers with the promise that I bring them back on Monday." He rocked his head back and forth. "I also have to give him a lap dance the next time I see him in the club."

Paris looked back at the coolers and then at Daniel. "We can't keep the food in coolers until the wedding."

"Terry is going to meet me at Grind House. They have space in their industrial freezer that we can store the food in," Daniel explained. "They also said I can use their kitchen to prep and cook the food."

Paris took his glasses off and massaged the bridge of his nose. "Why are they letting you do all that?"

"Terry and his boyfriends are the owners." Daniel winked at Paris. "They owe me."

Paris put his glasses back on. "At least Mark can't blame that on Daddy Twink."

"I am so tired of hearing about Daddy Twink," Daniel groaned. "Can we not mention him again the rest of the evening?"

Paris, realizing he was still holding Daniel's hand, gave it a squeeze. "Yeah."

"Good. I made you a plate. It's in the oven. I'll run the coolers over while you eat and get ready." Daniel gave him a quizzical look. "Do you have anything fun to wear tonight?"

157

Paris patted his messenger bag. "Oh, I think I have the perfect thing to wear." Standing up, Paris said, "Okay, let's get these coolers loaded up."

"I can do it by myself," Daniel declared, standing up.

Paris sat his bag down on the couch. "I didn't say you couldn't. So, are we going to get these coolers into your car, or are you going to strut around here like the biggest cock on the farm?"

"Well, I do have the—" Daniel started.

"Finish that sentence, and I'll put itching powder in your costumes," Paris warned. "Now, can we get on with it? I'm hungry."

Daniel winked at him. "Yeah, we can get it on."

"I can't believe you're wearing that shirt," Daniel laughed when they got into the back dressing room of Fae Boys. "It's so unlike you."

Paris did a little twirl. "I think a shirt that says, 'Daddy is my Bitch,' is the perfect shirt for me." He gave Daniel a sly smile. "Daddy."

"Fuck you." Daniel sat down at his station. "Can you help me lotion up?"

Not thinking anything of it, Paris said, "Sure."

"Great." Daniel stood and dropped his pants, revealing the bright yellow strap of a thong between his butt cheeks. "You can do my legs and back."

Paris caught Daniel's playful look in his reflection. He decided he wouldn't give Daniel the satisfaction of seeing him flustered. "Sure. Just make sure you wash this all off before we go to bed tonight. You don't want my cock accidentally slipping in."

"That's a bad thing?" Daniel asked, pulling off his shirt before passing Paris the lotion bottle.

Opening the bottle and crouching down, Paris said, "Depends on how you look at it."

"How do you look at it?" Daniel asked, rubbing lotion into his skin.

Paris hesitated a minute before moving up to rub lotion into Daniel's butt cheeks. "With a little bit of admiration. You must go to the gym a lot."

"Normally twice a day. In the morning, then at night," Daniel commented as he put lotion up his chest. "This week, I've just been going in the morning."

Rubbing lotion into Daniel's other cheek, Paris said, "I wouldn't know what to do in a gym."

"You're off tomorrow. Why don't you come with me in the morning?" Daniel groaned softly when Paris moved his hands up his back. "Since you invited me to sleep over and all."

Paris moved his hands over the muscular lines of Daniel's back. He hadn't realized that Daniel didn't need a place to crash since he had made up with his roommates. "I did drive us here, and you do get off pretty late. It only makes sense," Paris lied.

"There you go again, looking out for Daddy," Daniel teased.

FAE BOYS

"**Y**OU BROUGHT ME to Fae Boys?" Mark shouted over the music to Billy and Carlos. "You do know what we do for a living, right?"

Billy put a finger on the words across Mark's shirt. "Uh, yeah, sperm bank."

"Hey, there's a free spot at the bar. Let's get shots!" Carlos grabbed Mark's hand and pulled him through the crowd.

Mark smiled at the thought of alcohol. "I want something fruity and strong."

"Hunter's at his own bachelor party," Billy quipped. "Get us lemon drops."

Waiting behind the boys at the bar, Mark took a moment to scan the place. He smiled when he saw a familiar face sitting at the corner of the bar alone. He tapped Billy's shoulder and pointed. "We need another shot." Billy grinned when he saw who Mark was pointing at, then whispered to Carlos. He shouted to Billy, "I'll meet you over there!"

Mark slipped through the people drinking, laughing, and moving the beat of the thumping club music. Rounding the corner of the bar, he leaned into the ear of a distracted Paris and said, "So you'd rather sit in a bar by yourself than come out and hang out with your boss?"

"Holy shit!" Paris jumped, nearly spilling his drink. "What are you doing here?"

Mark put a hand on his shoulder. "This is where Billy and Carlos brought me."

"Shots!" Billy appeared with four tiny plastic cups in one hand and a drink in the other.

Handing one of the two drinks in his hands to Mark, Carlos said, "Looks like you are hanging out with us tonight, Paris!"

"You guys can't be here." Paris shot his eyes to the stage, then back to the three faces grinning at him.

Billy put a shot in Paris's hand. "Sure we can. It's Mark's bachelor's party!"

"Bottoms up, boys!" Mark raised his shot up.

Carlos raised his shot to Mark's and waited for everyone else to join. "To friendship, luck, and a really good fuck!"

"Seriously, you guys can't be here." Paris coughed after downing his drink.

Mark clasped Paris on the shoulder. "Why not? I'm getting married in what? Three days?"

"Four." Paris corrected before sipping his drink. He looked at the stage and saw Daniel coming out with the other go-go boys. Looking back at everyone, he said awkwardly. "Because Daniel is dancing on the bar tonight."

"That's why you didn't want to go out with us!" Billy exclaimed. "You wanted to see Daniel in his teeny weenie go-go boy boykini!"

Carlos nudged Billy. "It's a boykini, but it isn't teeny weenie."

"Jesus, how much is he packing?" Mark asked, wide-eyed.

Without thinking, Paris answered, "A lot."

"How do you know?" Mark asked, jostling Paris playfully.

Billy whispered loudly into Paris's ear. "Tell me you did your brothers proud and took all that."

"What? No! We just slept together. What I mean is he crashed at my place the last two nights," Paris said, flustered. "And I don't have any brothers."

Carlos put an arm around Billy. "Yes, you do. Us and Dennis."

"You've been officially adopted into the family," Mark patted his back. "That would make Hunter and me your dads."

Paris looked at them in disbelief. "Wow. I'm honored."

"So you know, you're our favorite." Mark kissed Paris on the cheek. "Don't tell your brothers."

Billy and Carlos looked at each other, then at Mark. In unison, they exclaimed, "Hey!"

"Hey, guys. Are you here to watch me dance?" Daniel asked, walking up.

Looking at each other again, Billy and Carlos exclaimed, "We are now!"

"I didn't know you danced here." Mark took a second to admire Daniel's trim and muscled body.

Daniel maneuvered his way to stand beside Paris. "I have a couple of side gigs."

Mark noticed Daniel slyly slipping a hand around Paris's waist. "Well, hopefully, you'll have time to make videos."

"Yeah." Daniel became noticeably uncomfortable. "Hey, Paris, David asked if you would help him, and one of the queens wanted to know if you could help her with her act."

Mark watched Paris casually slip a hand back around Daniel. "What does she need me to do?"

"She needs someone she can trust to handle her tips." Daniel smiled brightly at Paris. "After her performance, she has to bring some bachelor on stage, and one of us has to give him a lap dance."

Mark watched both of them grow wide-eyed and look at him. It took him a minute to catch on, then shout at Carlos and Billy, "What did you do?"

"Nothing, I swear," Billy said, playing innocent.

Carlos followed with, "I have no idea what you're talking about."

"I'll let you guys work that out. I got to get on the bar." Daniel pecked Paris on the cheek, then jumped up on the bar. Crouching down to the group, he said, "Don't have too much fun."

Mark found himself entranced by the sway of Daniel's hips and the swing of his extra-large schlong. "Boys, we got to tip him."

"I'm sure Paris already got the tip," Billy teased.

Carlos pulled out some money. "I think he got more than the tip; look at him."

163

"Paris, shut your mouth before someone sticks a dick in there." Billy reached over and tapped Paris's jaw closed.

Shaking off his awe, Paris said, "I should get in the back and see if they need any help."

"No, you don't." Mark trapped Paris between himself and the bar. "Boys." Carlos moved to one side, Billy the other. "I think it's time to tip this dancer."

Billy pulled out a twenty. "Yes, it is."

"I'm ready." Carlos began waving his twenty around.

"My boys always tip." Mark pulled out two twenties and put one in Paris's hand.

Crouching down, Daniel said, "Guys, you don't have to."

"Yes, we do!" Billy slipped his twenty into the side of Daniel's thong.

Tipping Daniel on the other side, Carlos said, "We'd be tipping even if it wasn't you."

"Come on, Paris." Mark nudged him forward, almost causing Paris to face plant into Daniel's crotch. He slipped the money in the front. "It's just a tip. You can handle a tip, right?"

Paris swallowed hard. He put the money in the front of Daniel's underwear. Before he could pull his hand back, Daniel grabbed it and rubbed it over his washboard stomach. Coyly, he asked loud enough for everyone to hear, "Is the lotion you rubbed all over me still on?"

"Yes." Paris sounded out of breath when he answered.

Letting go of Paris's hand, Daniel said, "I need to work the bar. Meet you back here on my loop?"

"Of course," Mark answered for him.

Paris waited for Daniel to stand and start moving around the bar before he said, "I really should head to the back."

"Meet us back here?" Billy asked. "We'll try to behave."

Paris nodded. "Yeah. I definitely will."

"We won't behave," Mark admitted, showing off the words "Sperm Bank" across his chest. "But, please, come back."

"Awe, they make such a cute couple!" Carlos exclaimed when Paris left. "I wonder if they have pet names for each other."

Putting a hand on Billy's and Carlos's shoulders. "They aren't a couple." Mark grinned devilishly. "Yet." He pulled them close. "Boys, you're going to help me change that tonight."

LAP DANCE STRIP TEASE

PARIS PEEKED THROUGH the curtains at Mark on stage with Bonita Flores. When she specifically called Mark up onto the stage, Billy and Carlos pushed him up. The crowd was cheering for Mark while he flexed in his "Sperm Bank" shirt and Bonita Flores was feeling his muscles.

"Hey, Paris, thanks again for helping me with my outfit." David, one of Terry's boyfriends and Daniel's other roommate, patted him on the back.

He was the last person Paris expected to be a go-go boy. He was chubby, with a hairy chest and a reddish brown beard. The people seemed to love him, because he had stacks of crumbled and sweaty bills, just like Daniel. He definitely was entertaining to watch flirt with the clientele.

"No problem. I can't believe you wear those wings on the bar." Paris laughed, turning his attention away from Mark.

David smiled guiltily at Paris. "I know Daniel said everything was forgiven and to not mention it, but my boyfriends and I are really sorry about Tweeting that the other day. I hope it didn't cause too much trouble."

"Tweeting what?" Paris asked, confused.

Daniel suddenly appeared by David's side. "Hey, David, go grab me a chair to take out on stage, please."

"Sure." David slinked off.

"What was he talking about?" Paris asked.

"Here you go," David said, returning with a folding chair, then leaving.

"What Tweet?" Paris repeated.

Daniel shook his head. "It was nothing. Look, he's finally stopped preening."

"Are you really going to give him a lap dance?" Paris looked out to see Mark standing proudly next to Bonita Flores.

Bonita Flores spoke into the microphone. "Honey, you're getting married, and you're walking around with 'Sperm Bank' on your shirt?"

"I'm getting married, not dying," Mark answered into the microphone.

Bonita feigned indignation. "Oh, my. What does your future husband think about that?"

"He watched me get fucked by those two the last two days." Mark pointed at Billy and Carlos.

Bonita put a hand over her heart. "My, my, my. You must have a fantastic job for him to be okay with this. What do you do for work, honey?"

"I'm an adult film actor." The crowd erupted in catcalls from the audience. Mark stopped Bonita from pulling away the microphone. "So is my husband."

Bonita waved for Daniel to come out while she waited for the crowd to quiet down. "Your sexy friends over there arranged for you to have a lap dance by our hottest dancer, our very own daddy twink, Daniel!"

Paris saw Mark bristle at the mention of the name. Daniel moved out onto the stage, wearing just a black jock. Daniel stuck his ass out to the crowd as he opened the chair and sat it on the stage. Giving the crowd a shake of his ass, Daniel moved behind the chair and waited for Mark to sit down.

"I have a feeling you know this sexy little stud here." Bonita ran a hand down Daniel's arm.

Mark gleefully answered, "I do. He works for me."

"He's not the only one that works for you, is he? I understand my new favorite pocket gay does, too." Bonita turned to the curtain Paris was peeking out. "Paris! Paris France! Could you come out here, please?!"

Hands from behind pushed Paris through the curtain. He froze. "Come on out here, baby. I don't bite." Bonita paused. "Hard."

Paris stood there frozen in the spotlight with every eye in the club on him. His heart was pounding in his ears. His palms were sweaty. He wanted to turn around and rush back into the back room. He willed his legs to move in any direction, but they wouldn't obey. A strong, familiar hand took his.

"I got you." It was Daniel. He led Paris down to the center of the stage.

Gushing, Bonita smiled at them. "Don't they make a cute couple?!"

"Don't they?" Mark said devilishly.

Bonita turned to Mark and said, "Well, I guess it's not appropriate for your employee to give you a lap dance. This isn't one of your movies."

"No." The crowd began to boo at Mark's answer. "Paris is my personal assistant. Maybe he could fill in?" The crowd began to cheer.

Before Paris could run away, Bonita sat Paris down on the chair. "What a wonderful idea!"

"Oh, shit," Paris mouthed, realizing what was about to happen.

Bonita escorted Mark to the side of the stage where Billy and Carlos were standing. "DJ, can we get some bump and grind music? Daniel! Do your thing!"

"I'm so sorry. I didn't know." Paris's vision cleared when a body blocked the spotlight that had been blinding him. It was Daniel speaking to him. "You can just sit there. I'll do all the work."

Paris wasn't sure if this was really happening or if he was dreaming. Daniel was straddling him. Daniel's hips were moving in his lap. Daniel had his arms looped around his head. Daniel's jock-covered cock was rubbing all over his shirt. There was something off with Daniel, like he was nervous.

"Come on, Daniel!" Bonita's voice boomed around them. "Make it spicier! You can do it, Daddy!"

Paris saw it in Daniel's shadowed face, felt it in his stiff movements. He was floundering in front of a club full of people. Remembering how Daniel moved in his living room and on the bar, Paris knew Daniel could do better. He was holding back. He needed a little push. Paris pushed.

169

Leaning forward into Daniel's chest, Paris's hands came around him to slowly move up along his back. He felt a slight tremor in Daniel's body. Loud enough for only Daniel to hear, he said, "It's just me and you here. Forget everyone else."

Paris felt the tension leave Daniel, but his movements were still stiff. Paris heard Mark and the others shouting at them, but he couldn't make out the words. He was focused on Daniel. Daniel needed him. He had to do something to get Daniel out of his head. Paris didn't like it, but he knew what he had to do.

"You're leaving me no choice," Paris warned.

Paris didn't know where the courage came from when he stood up and sent Daniel stumbling back. Paris whipped his glasses off and tossed them toward Mark and the others. He looked at Daniel standing confused in the spotlight. Right as Paris took Daniel's hand and pulled Daniel behind him, the music cut off.

Bonita's sassy voice boomed through the speakers. "If you don't turn that music back on, I will personally come up to your DJ booth and shove my size thirteen heel up your ass."

The music started back up. Paris pulled Daniel flush with his back. He took Daniel's hands and put them on his hips. He ground his ass into Daniel's cloth-covered crotch. He felt Daniel start to move with him. Daniel's fingers fisted the bottom of his shirt. Paris leaned his head back to rest it on Daniel's shoulder.

Lost in the moment, Paris raised his hands above his head and whispered, "Come on, Daddy, show your boy what you got."

170

Daniel pulled Paris's shirt out from his pants, then up along his body. Paris felt the warm air of the bar touch his exposed skin. Daniel pulled the shirt off and tossed it away. He put his hands on Paris's chest. He moved them slowly down Paris's body to the top of his pants. Daniel popped open the top of Paris's pants.

"Looks like this lap dance turned into a little strip tease!" Bonita announced.

He reached into Paris's pants with one hand. He groped Paris's hardening cock. With his other hand, he ran it slowly across Paris's chest. "Do you trust me?" He growled into Paris's ear.

Breathless, Paris answered, "Yes."

"Hold on to my hands tightly," Daniel ordered, moving his hands to take Paris's. "I got you."

Daniel lifted Paris's hands up above his head. Daniel spun him around, swiped his feet from under him, and then lowered Paris carefully to the floor. Daniel fell on top of Paris, holding himself inches away from Paris. He whipped his body in waves along Paris's. He stared into Paris's eyes. Paris thought he saw something in Daniel's eyes.

Then Daniel was up, pulling Paris along with him. Paris's back was to the crowd. Daniel turned and began wiggling his ass against him. When he turned around, Paris thought Daniel was about to kiss him. The music ended. The moment ended, and Daniel pulled away. Paris quickly did up his pants.

"Bitches, you weren't turned on by that!" Bonita exclaimed over the speakers. "You're dead!"

Mark came over and handed Paris back his shirt. He whispered to Paris, "That was hot." Paris slipped

171

on his shirt. Putting Paris's glasses back on his face, Mark said, "That boy likes you. If you don't see that, you need a new prescription."

31

THIS COFFEE IS HORRIBLE

MARK WINCED AT the light attacking his closed eyes. His head throbbed. His mouth felt like sandpaper. He was hot and cold at the same time. Even the slightest movement seemed like a monumental task. If he could get five more minutes of sleep, he'd be okay. The problem was, his bladder was screaming for release.

Mark pulled Hunter close to him, except it wasn't Hunter. The body was too small and muscular. Then he realized someone was snoring behind him. What did he do last night? Did he and the boys bring people back from the bar? Did they go home with people? It was all hazy after the show ended.

Mark forced his eyes open. His blurry vision cleared. He instantly felt relief to see he was holding Billy in his bed. He looked over his shoulder to see Carlos on his back, mouth agape, snoring like a chainsaw. Between the pain of needing to piss and Carlos's snoring, Mark decided he had to get up.

Careful not to disturb the slumbering boys, Mark slipped out of bed, only to nearly fall back down when he stood too fast. He heard the sheets rustle. He turned to watch a sleeping Billy move until he latched onto Carlos. He pulled the boy until Carlos was spooning him, silencing the snores.

With that daunting task done, Mark stumbled naked to the bathroom. He sat down on the toilet, knowing better than to try to aim on swaying legs. He dropped his head into his hands and moaned in relief as the pressure in his bladder eased. Once he was done, he had the urge to curl up on the cold tile floor and fall back asleep.

How did we end up naked in bed together? Mark wondered. *Where's Hunter?*

Mark forced himself to stand up, grabbing the vanity to keep himself from falling over. He looked into the mirror. He groaned in anguish when he saw his reflection. His hair was every which way where it wasn't matted down. His face looked pale and clammy, with dark rings under his eyes.

Turning on the faucet, Mark splashed cold water onto his face. He felt a little better. He cupped some water into his hand and brought it to his parched mouth. He looked over at the shower. He was pretty sure he stank of the club and booze. He needed to get clean and get on with his day. He'd had fun last night, but today he needed to do wedding stuff.

Stepping into the shower, Mark turned on the water, enjoying the cold water shocking his system. He put his face into the stream and felt the filth trickling down his body. When the water warmed, Mark grabbed the body wash and started scrubbing himself. He was beginning to feel like a human being again.

Toweling off, Mark felt refreshed. He still had that annoying throb in his head, but two aspirin would hopefully fix that. Stepping back into the bedroom, he saw his clothes scattered around the room with Billy's and Carlos's. He pulled a clean pair of shorts and a shirt from his drawers. After quietly slipping them on, he looked through his pants to find his phone.

It was badly in need of a charge. Mark quickly checked his phone calls and text. He had drunk-dialed and texted Hunter at least thirty times, but there was no response. A nervous pit formed in Mark's stomach. He called Hunter but was sent right to voicemail right before the phone screen flickered out with a battery icon demanding to be attended to.

Mark put the phone on the charger on his night-stand, then slinked out of the room. He thought he heard Billy and Carlos stirring, but he didn't have time for that. He called out, "Hunter!" There was no answer. Mark checked Dennis and Benjamin's room. The bed was made, but they weren't there.

"Dennis!" Mark called out frantically. "Benjamin!"

Mark flew into the kitchen. The coffee was made. That put him a little at ease. *Where is everyone?* He reached for his phone, then remembered it was charging. He looked out the window to see Dennis and Benjamin coming out of the guest house. Another wave of ease hit him. *They must have been talking to Brad and Cody.* Mark waited to see if Hunter would appear. *Come on, Hunter. This isn't funny.*

"Hey, sleepyhead." Dennis smiled brightly, walking in. "Are the other two still comatose?"

Panicked, Mark demanded, "Where is Hunter? Why didn't he answer any of my calls or texts?"

"Calm down, Mark." Benjamin stepped in front of Dennis.

Mark growled angrily, "Where is Hunter?"

"He took your car to go pick up Lexi and Ryan from the airport. Let me call him." Dennis pulled out his phone. Putting it to his ear, he frowned. "Voicemail. I'm going to connect his phone to your car before we leave."

Mark crumbled to the floor. "I'm sorry. I'm hungover. I haven't had my coffee. My head hurts."

"I'll get the coffee." Dennis bolted to the counter.

Benjamin moved to the cabinets. "Aspirin. You need aspirin."

"Why didn't Hunter answer my calls or texts last night?" Mark cried out.

Dennis kneeled down and put a fresh cup of coffee in his hand. "You guys came home sloppy drunk last night."

"We were here, and you kept asking, 'Where is Hunter?'" Benjamin pressed two aspirin into his hand.

Teary-eyed, Mark asked, "Where was he?"

"He was right there in front of you." Dennis tried not to laugh when he answered. "You kept texting him and calling him. When we told you he was Hunter, you yelled, 'No, you're not! You're working with Daddy Twink!' Then you, Billy, and Carlos disappeared into the bedroom to make a plan to rescue him."

"I'm so sorry." Mark popped the pills in his mouth and chased them with coffee. "This coffee is horrible."

Dennis pointed at Benjamin. "He made it."

"Liar." Benjamin playfully shoved Dennis. Turning serious, Benjamin said, "Hunter filled us in on the Daddy Twink thing."

Mark shook his head. "I know I'm overreacting." Mark took a sip of coffee and made a face. "Seriously, this is horrible coffee. Help me up so I can make a decent pot."

"You're not overreacting." Benjamin pulled Mark to his feet. "Considering our history. Did Paris find out anything about him?"

Mark dumped the coffee out of the pot. He huffed. "No, but he's been busy putting out fires with the wedding, getting this project with Lexi off the ground, and flirting with Daniel."

"Daniel," Dennis said with interest. "The sexy cooking twink."

Mark scooped coffee into the maker. "Yes, Daniel, the sexy cooking twink."

"You're not filming with him." Benjamin quickly informed Dennis.

Mark poured water into the maker. "Daniel doesn't film. He cleans our house. We hired him to cook this past week, and he apparently is a go-go boy at Fae Boys."

"I told you we should have gone with them," Dennis pouted.

Benjamin rolled his eyes. "You see how they look this morning."

"It would have been worth it." Dennis grinned.

Mark chuckled, then winced. "It was, especially when Paris turned his lap dance into a striptease."

"Paris did a lap dance?" Benjamin balked.

Mark turned around and leaned against the counter. "No, Daniel did the lap dance. Paris did the striptease."

"You better have recorded it or at least took pictures," Dennis sulked.

Mark gave Dennis a regretful look. "Sorry. Maybe Billy or Carlos did?"

"He doesn't need to see it anyway. He's got me." Benjamin pulled Dennis into a hug. "Oh, Hunter told us to remind you that you're going to pick up your tuxes you two forgot to pick up yesterday after you stop by the venue to give them the final check."

Mark smiled. "It's really happening, isn't it?"

I AM NOT A SIZE QUEEN!

"**I** NEED A SHOWER," Paris groaned when they entered his apartment. "It's official. I hate exercise."

Shutting the door behind them, Daniel laughed. "You did great."

"I'm sweaty and nasty." Paris dramatically fell on the couch.

Daniel went to the kitchen. "Quit being dramatic. I'm going to make us lunch, and if you're a good boy, I'll give you a massage."

"Fine." Paris smiled to himself. They hadn't talked about their show at the club last night. When he woke up with Daniel in his arms, he casually ran his hand up and down Daniel's chest. He remembered Daniel's words to him, *I got you.* Then he remembered Mark telling him how obvious it was Daniel was interested in him.

"Why are you so quiet?" Daniel asked from the kitchen.

Paris sat up and watched Daniel cooking. He remembered what Dennis had told him about the cooking show. "Shit."

"What?" Daniel perked up.

Paris stood up and walked over to the kitchen. "Please, don't be mad."

"Mad about what?" Daniel asked suspiciously.

Paris rubbed his hands together nervously. "I did something you're not going to be happy about."

"What did you do?" Daniel stopped what he was doing to look at Paris.

Paris took in a deep breath and blurted it out. "I sent the video of you cooking to Lexi Luscious, and now she wants you and me to do a cooking show for her streaming service."

"You what!" Daniel exclaimed. Paris closed his eyes and prepared for Daniel's inevitable tirade. Arms came around him, and he was lifted up into the air. "I know I made a big deal about you filming me, but thank you! I could kiss you!"

Opening his eyes, Paris looked into Daniel's smiling eyes. He pressed his lips to Daniel's. There was a moment of shock on Daniel's face, then he kissed back. Paris felt the floor under his feet. Daniel let go of Paris. Paris moved his hands to the small of Daniel's back to keep him close

Without warning, Daniel pulled away. He glared angrily at Paris. "Why did you do that?"

"You said you could kiss me." Paris looked at him, confused. "I thought you liked me, I mean, after last night and what Mark said."

Daniel shook his head in disbelief. "I do, but you don't like me. Not really."

"What are you talking about?" Paris asked in disbelief. "I do like you."

Daniel gave Paris an incredulous look. "You didn't pay me any attention until you saw I had a big dick like Daddy Twink. Face it, Paris, you're a size queen."

"What?!" Paris slapped Daniel across the face. "I am not a size queen."

Daniel rubbed his stinging cheek. "Bullshit. Look how obsessed you are with Daddy Twink."

"Only because of that note that Mark is freaking out about," Paris said vehemently, "I can't believe you after all the time we spent together this week."

Daniel crossed his arms. "How many of Daddy Twink's videos have you watched?"

"A lot, but that was research," Paris defended. "I was trying to figure out who he is."

Daniel's eyes were filled with anger and hurt. "Do you want to know who Daddy Twink is? Do you? I am."

"You are not," Paris scoffed.

Daniel dropped his shorts and jock. He took his cock in hand and showed Paris the mole. "Yes, I am!"

"Asshole!" Paris slapped Daniel's cheek again. "Do you know what you put Mark through? What were you thinking?!"

Daniel rubbed his cheek. "I know! I'm sorry! Now will you … please … stop … slapping me or at least start slapping the other side?"

"Fine!" Paris slapped the other cheek. "That's for thinking I'd be so shallow to be only interested in you for your dick! Impressive as it is, it's not going in me!"

Daniel shouted back, "Good! I prefer to bottom anyway!"

"Really?" Paris asked curiously, lowering his voice. "You top in all your videos."

Daniel shrugged. "People want to see a big dick guy top, not get fucked."

"True," Paris conceded. "Where does this leave us?"

Daniel laughed. "It leaves me with my dick hanging out in your kitchen."

"It also leaves our lunch burning." Paris pointed to the stove.

Daniel whipped around and moved the pan off the stove. "Shit!"

"It's okay." Paris wrapped his arms around Daniel's waist from behind. "I don't think I'm hungry for food anymore."

Turning off the stove, Daniel turned in his arms. "Oh? What are you hungry for?"

"You." Paris kissed him

Daniel ran a hand through Paris's sweaty hair. "Sounds good," Daniel smirked. "But you're taking a shower first. You stink."

"Join me." Paris's question came out a command.

Freshly showered and barely dried off, Paris and Daniel fell onto the bed in a tangle of limbs as they kissed. In the shower, they had resisted every urge to ravage each other, choosing to explore one another's familiar bodies instead as they washed each other until the water ran cold. They were clean; now they wanted to get dirty.

"I've wanted this for so long," Daniel groaned while Paris kissed along his neck.

Paris growled in his ear, "I've wanted this all week."

"What?" Daniel rolled them over so he was on top. "Just this week? I've been working at the house for months!"

Paris rolled them over again. He straddled Daniel's waist and pinned his hands above his head. "I was always working, and you were always cleaning." Paris grinned. "I sort of had a fantasy about you like this. Remember when you washed my pants?"

"Mm, yeah, they were soaked," Daniel purred. "Tell me about it."

Paris leaned down and whispered in his ear. "It was about Daddy Twink, but when I blew my load, I saw your face." Daniel squirmed under him. "Want to know more?"

"Yes," Daniel urged him, lust dripping from his voice.

"Why tell you, when I can show you?" Paris pulled back, a lecherous grin on his face. "I did learn something from working for adult film performers."

Licking his lips, Daniel ordered, "Show me."

"Yes, Daddy," Paris said seductively.

Keeping Daniel's hands pinned, Paris leaned down to gently kiss Daniel's left nipple. Daniel gasped, then groaned and writhed when Paris circled his tongue around the sensitive flesh. Daniel's breath hitched and his body tensed at the feel of Paris's teeth softly nibbling on the nub.

"I love hearing you moan," Paris said, pausing to quickly kiss Daniel before heading to the right nipple.

Daniel's body tensed. Paris felt Daniel restrain himself from breaking free of his grasp. "Paris," Daniel half moaned, half whimpered. "Oh, Paris."

"Don't move," Paris ordered. "Or else."

Trying to catch his breath, Daniel asked, "Or else what?"

"You won't get to see what happens next," Paris threatened.

Letting his hands slide along Daniel's arms, Paris adorned his body with kisses, tracing the lines of his muscles with his tongue. Paris drew graffiti doodles across his washboard abs, wrote his name along Daniel's left side, and Bitch Daddy along his right. Whenever he found a sensitive spot, Paris attacked it.

Daniel jerked with every brush and swipe of Paris's tongue. He repeated Paris's name over and over again in moans, groans, and pleas. His body shook and spasmed with pleasure, but he kept his hands where they were. Paris could tell Daniel was using every ounce of restraint to quell the urge and impulse to move.

Paris ran an exploratory hand from the base of Daniel's elephantine cock to the tip. He felt its heat as it pulsed under his gliding fingertips. Thick and hard, Daniel's cock looked much bigger and more intimidating up close than it had in the videos, with his fat head dribbling pre-cum. Paris hefted the thirteen-inch pole up toward the sky.

"Paris, you don't—" Daniel's words were turned into a gasp when Paris licked around the crown, then

ran zigzag patterns down to Daniel's hairless balls. "Paris, please! Oh! God!"

Pushing Daniel's legs apart, Paris took one hefty ball in his mouth, then the other. He heard Daniel thrash against his imaginary bonds. He licked up the length of Daniel's cock, then back down, past Daniel's balls, to the sensitive spot down below. He flicked his tongue. Daniel let out a restrained moan.

Paris sat up on his knees between Daniel's legs. He watched Daniel's chest heaving. "There's more, but I have to build up to that," Paris said impishly. "I guess I should improvise the rest."

Paris lifted Daniel's legs and curled the surprised man into a ball. He flicked his tongue into Daniel's hole. He circled his tongue along the rim, then brushed his tongue up and down the smooth crack. Paris could feel him opening up. It almost felt like Daniel was trying to pull him in.

Paris lowered Daniel's legs, licking up along his cock again as he did. Daniel's nostrils were flared. He had a wild look in his eyes. The moment his legs hit the bed, Daniel pounced on Paris. Tumbling around in the bed, they kissed and explored each other's bodies until Daniel ended up on top.

"Daddy's turn," Daniel snarled.

Paris danced his fingers over Daniel's back, making him arch from the pleasure. "I thought I was in charge."

"I'm improvising." Daniel kissed Paris deeply. "I want you to fuck me so badly, but first."

Daniel kissed his way down Paris's chest and stomach to his hard cock. He looked up to watch

Paris as he slurped him down. Moaning, Paris ran his hands through Daniel's hair. He arched his hips up, thrusting his cock into Daniel's mouth. The two fell into a rhythm, with Daniel meeting every one of Paris's pumps into his mouth.

Pulling off him. Daniel said, "Daddy needs that dick inside him."

"Gladly." Paris grinned.

Daniel flipped onto his back and pulled his legs to his chest. Grabbing the lube from his nightstand, Paris drizzled lube over Daniel's hole. He pressed one finger, then two, into Daniel, scissoring his fingers to prepare him for the stretch. When he couldn't wait anymore, he positioned himself between Daniel's legs and pushed in.

"Paris, you feel so good inside me," Daniel moaned.

Paris grabbed Daniel's ankles. "It feels amazing to be in you."

Paris rotated his hips with every pump into Daniel. He kept his pace slow and steady, enjoying the feel of Daniel around his cock. He leaned forward, resting Daniel's legs on his shoulders. Staring into Daniel's eyes, he picked up his speed slightly. He felt Daniel's hands on his back, pulling him forward. Paris kissed him.

They shifted positions, moving to their sides. With his chest pressed to Daniel's back, Paris lifted Daniel's leg and slid back in. Daniel turned his head to kiss Paris while he pumped his cock. Paris's mouth moved to suck on the soft skin of Daniel's neck. Gasping, Daniel reached back to grab Paris's head.

Daniel rolled Paris onto his back. He straddled Paris and lowered himself onto Paris's hard cock. Daniel leaned back and began riding Paris. Paris poured lube into his hand, then grabbed Daniel's big flopping cock. Daniel fucked Paris's hand while fucking himself on Paris's cock. Daniel began moving faster. Paris met his downward movements.

"I'm going to cum, Daniel," Paris warned. Daniel flexed his ass muscles as he rode Paris harder. "Daniel," Paris said through clenched teeth.

"Cream inside of me," Daniel growled. "Fucking cream my insides, boy."

Daniel's command set Paris off. He began jack-hammering his hips up into Daniel. "Take it, Daddy." Paris's body shuddered as his cock began spraying inside Daniel. "Take it! Take it!" Paris's body went rigid, then limp with the release.

"Mm, baby." Daniel slipped off of Paris and lay beside him. "Kiss me." He began stroking his cock. Paris slipped his tongue into Daniel's mouth. He reached down between Daniel's legs. He slipped two fingers back into Daniel. A few moments later, Daniel began whimpering. Then he thrust his hips up, shooting his load high up into the air and splattering down on them.

Paris gentled the kiss. He pulled his fingers out and ran his hands up and over Daniel's chest. "How's my daddy feeling?'

"Like I need another shower." Daniel laughed. "You did learn something working for adult film stars."

Paris patted Daniel's chest. "Just a little something." He kissed Daniel. "Promise me this wasn't a one-time thing?"

"No, it wasn't," Daniel answered, running his hands through Paris's hair. "You, I don't know, make me nervous. I'm normally really confident with guys."

Paris rubbed his nose against Daniel's. "I make you nervous?"

"Yeah, you're so smart and sexy." Daniel pulled Paris onto his cum covered chest. "And covered in spunk!"

Paris wriggled away. "Jerk!" Paris tapped his chest. "Go get the shower ready. I want to check my phone."

"Kiss your Daddy." Daniel grinned.

Paris gave Daniel a quick peck. "You're forgetting, 'Daddy's my Bitch.'" Paris pulled away and slipped off the bed. "Go on, get the shower ready."

"Wash my back and I'll wash yours," Daniel joked, getting off the bed. He saw the concerned look on Paris's face. "What's wrong?"

Looking up from his phone, "Hunter sent me a text. He needs me over there right away."

"Did he say why?" Daniel asked, moving to Paris's side.

"No." Paris put an arm around Daniel. "Something bad must have happened."

Daniel patted Paris's bare ass. "Text him we're on our way. I'll start the shower."

"You don't," Paris started, then saw the look on Daniel's face. "Sent."

33

MARK'S MELTDOWN

"**I CAN'T BELIEVE THIS** is happening!" Mark screamed hysterically as he paced in the living room. He didn't care that he was losing it in front of everyone. "All I want to do is get married!"

Hunter caught him in a bear hug. "Mark, calm down. We'll figure this out."

"Then what?" Mark broke free of Hunter's hold. "We'll figure this out, and then Daddy Twink will do something else to sabotage our wedding!"

Speaking up from the couch, Dennis said, "We don't know it was Daddy Twink."

"Who is Daddy Twink?" Ryan whispered to Carlos.

Mark scowled at Ryan. "Who is Daddy Twink?! I'll tell you who Daddy Twink is!" he yelled maniacally. "He's the want-to-be porn actor that has been sabotaging our wedding!"

"That really doesn't answer the question," Ryan whispered to Carlos.

Lexi shot him a look. "Not now, Ryan."

"It would be nice to have some frame of reference so I know what's going on," Ryan defended, fluttering his hand.

Mark trembled when he spoke. "He had one of his—what are they called?"

"Service Boys," Carlos answered. When everyone looked at him, he shrugged. "Paris showed us the video. It was hot."

Billy nodded. "It was."

"Can I get a copy?" Ryan asked.

Lexi quietly said, "Send me a copy, too."

"Guys, not the time," Hunter growled.

Mark seethed. "I'm glad you guys want to get off on watching the guy who is trying to destroy my life!"

"He's not trying to destroy your life," Hunter said calmly.

Mark's nostrils flared with anger. "One of his Service Boys almost ran us over with his car!"

"Todd explained everything," Hunter defended. "He was driving carelessly when he almost hit you, and he filmed with Daddy Twink once. That doesn't mean Daddy Twink was involved or that he's trying to sabotage our wedding."

Dennis, Billy, and Carlos said in chorus, "Well…"

"Not helping," Hunter growled.

Mark continued, "Then our caterer is murdered, and it's made to look like an accident!"

"Michael is under arrest for that," Hunter amended.

Mark threw up his arms in frustration. "Then how do you explain that the place we were going to have our wedding was burned down last night?!"

"I…" Hunter shook his head. "I don't know. Look, can we all stop jumping to conclusions until we know something?" Hunter pulled out his ringing phone. "It's Caleb. Maybe he knows something." Putting the phone to his ear, he said, "Caleb. Please tell me you have something."

Everyone was quiet while Hunter listened to Caleb on the phone. "Okay, thank you. We'll see you soon." Hunter put his phone away. Soberly, he looked at Mark. "It was arson. They are trying to pull the security footage now."

"I told you it was Daddy Twink!" Mark shrieked.

Paris and Daniel appeared in the doorway. "What was Daddy Twink?" Paris asked.

"Daddy Twink burned down our wedding venue!" Mark proclaimed.

Paris and Daniel exchanged glances. Defensively, Daniel asked, "Why do you think Daddy Twink did it?"

"It all started when he sent us that flash drive with the threatening note!" Mark held up a finger. "He filmed with that muscled boy that almost hit me with a car." Mark held up another finger. "Then our caterer is murdered." Mark held up a third finger. "That nasty ass tweet!" Mark held up a fourth finger. "Now our venue has been burned down." Mark held up his thumb. "Not to mention, we don't know who he is, and we can't find him so he can explain himself."

"It wasn't Daddy Twink," Paris insisted.

Hunter stepped in. "Paris, Caleb told me the police want to question him. If you know anything, please tell me."

"Why do they think that?" Daniel spat out angrily. "Because you told them it was him?"

Paris pulled Daniel into his arms. "Daniel, calm down. It'll be okay."

"Oh my God!" Billy exclaimed. "They had sex!"

Carlos's eyes grew wide with excitement. "They did! Paris, tell me you took all that dick!"

"Guys!" Hunter reprimanded.

Billy whined, "But Hunter, you don't know how big Daniel's dick is."

"Can we not talk about Daniel's enormous dick right now?!" Mark screamed.

Ryan raised his hand. "Will we be circling back to the twunk and his enormous dick?"

"I sure hope so." Lexi looked Daniel up and down. "I'm dying to know how Paris took that big dick."

Dennis nodded to Paris. "Much respect, dude. I heard about his package."

"I bottomed for him." Daniel spat out, pulling away from Paris.

Lexi, Ryan, Dennis, Carlos, and Billy simultaneously said, "Respect."

"Guys, please, Mark is freaking out here." Benjamin finally spoke. "Can we, please, focus on the problem at hand?" He looked to Paris. "Paris, how do you know Daddy Twink wasn't involved in the fire last night?"

Paris looked at Daniel, who gave him a nod. "Because I know where he was last night." Paris paused. "You all do."

"What are you talking about?" Mark asked.

Paris took a deep breath. "Because you all watched him on stage with me last night."

"He was on stage with Daniel last night." A confused Billy said to Carlos.

Carlos thought for a moment. "It wasn't the Drag Queen, was it?"

"Who else was on stage with him?" Dennis asked.

"I'm Daddy Twink," Daniel announced. "I couldn't have burned down the venue because I was waving the big dick you're all obsessed with around on stage for you."

Hunter quickly moved to stop a charging Mark. "Mark, don't."

"You're fucking Daddy Twink!" Mark screeched. "Why are you trying to ruin my wedding!?"

Daniel stood, ready to fight. "I'm not trying to ruin your wedding. In fact, I'm the one cooking for it!"

"Daniel," Paris took his hand, "maybe we should go. Wait until everyone calms down and talk about this, then."

Mark struggled in Hunter's arms. "The fuck I'd eat your poisoned food! You're fired! I never want to see you in this house again!"

"Mark," Hunter warned. "Don't say anything you might regret later."

Paris looked at a seething Daniel, then at an enraged Mark. "If he's not welcome here, then neither am I."

"Paris, Mark doesn't mean what he's saying. Please, don't," Hunter pleaded.

Mark spat out, "Fine, you're fired. Get your shit and go!"

"Mark!" Hunter pushed Mark back away from the two boys. "Enough!"

193

Paris tugged on Daniel's hand. "It's fine. We'll go." Paris shook his head. "So much for being part of the family. I'll make arrangements to get my things."

"Paris, please, don't," Hunter called after a retreating Paris and Daniel. Lowering his head, he turned around and fixed his angry gaze on Mark. "I hope you're fucking happy!"

"Why are you mad at me?!" Mark shouted back.

Hunter shook his head. "You were expecting this wedding to be ruined. Well, congratulations. You just ruined it."

"I didn't do anything!" Mark defended. "It was all Daniel or Daddy Twink or whatever he calls himself!"

Hunter sighed. "Believe that if you must."

"I can still marry the two of you," Ryan interjected quietly.

Hunter sighed. "Thanks, but I don't think I want to get married anymore." Hunter turned and walked out of the room.

"Hunter!" Mark cried out. Dennis and Benjamin quickly moved to hug him. "Hunter!"

Dennis patted Mark's back. "Give him some time. I'll talk to him."

"Hunter!" Mark crumbled to the floor in tears.

PUTTING THE PIECES TOGETHER

WRAPPED IN DANIEL'S arms, Paris lay on his couch. *What did I do?* He pulled Daniel's arm tighter around him. His phone had finally stopped going off with notifications of phone calls and text messages. He was sure his voicemail was full of messages he didn't want to hear, at least not right now.

"Are you okay?" Daniel pulled him closer to him. "You didn't have to quit over me."

Paris ran his fingers over the top of Daniel's hands. "I didn't quit because of you." Paris sighed. "Well, not just because of you. Mark was being unreasonable."

"He was upset," Daniel said soothingly. "I shouldn't have popped off like that. It didn't help matters."

Paris interlaced his fingers with Daniel's. "No, but... I don't know. Things got out of hand."

"I wonder who set fire to the venue." Daniel squeezed Paris's hand. "Where was the wedding going to be at? I don't think you told me."

Paris laughed. "Rainbow Unicorn Kitty Hall."

"Where?" Daniel asked, shifting on the couch.

Paris chuckled. "I know. It's such an absurd name. Can you believe someone named it that?"

"Yes." Daniel grew serious. "Michael owns it."

Paris looked at him, confused. "The one that died?"

"No, fuck. Okay, for now, we're calling them Dead Michael and Alive Michael," Daniel declared. "Dead Michael ran the catering company. Alive Michael ran the venue for weddings and whatnot. To rent the Alive Michael's venue, you had to use Dead Michael as the caterer."

Paris thought for a moment. "Dead Michael is the one that suggested Rainbow Unicorn Kitty Hall."

"Right, they were making a killing by sending each other clientele." Daniel winced. "Poor choice of words."

Paris mauled over Daniel's words. "Then who-ever it was, wasn't trying to ruin Hunter's and Mark's wedding. They were trying to ruin Dead Michael and Alive Michael's lives."

"Right." Daniel shifted them so they were sitting. "Who would be crazy enough to kill?"

Paris then asked, "And how is that muscled boy you filmed with involved?"

"Right, Mark said I filmed with him. Do you remember which video?" Daniel asked. "I didn't get a look when you pulled it up on your computer."

Paris picked up his phone and cringed at the dozens of notifications on his phone. Ignoring them, he pulled up Daddy Twink's fan site. "Yeah, let me see. This one." He held the phone for Daniel to see. "Do you remember him?"

"Remember that psycho? Yeah. He works, or worked, with me at M and M catering," Daniel answered.

Paris pulled the phone back. "What do you mean 'psycho?'"

"After we filmed, he hounded Terry to find out who I was because he was in love with me. I found out three of his exes had restraining orders on him." Daniel rolled his eyes. "He's the obsessive type." Daniel thought for a moment. "You know, I got the vibe that Dead Michael and he were fucking."

Paris looked at his phone. "You don't think?"

"Dead Michael broke up with him, and then Todd poisoned him?" Daniel clarified. "It's a distinct possibility."

Paris thought for a second. "What about the venue, though? Why would he burn that down?"

"Maybe they were both fucking him?" Daniel shrugged. "It's worth checking out. Do you know anyone who might be able to put these pieces together for us?"

Paris looked at the contacts in his phone. "Yeah, the guy fucking Todd right now." Paris hit Caleb's number. "Hey, Caleb. It's Paris."

"Paris, where the fuck are you?" Caleb barked through the phone. "This place is a madhouse. Hunter is locked in his room and won't come out. Mark is crying in the kitchen. Shit, I know they said some things, but we need you here."

Paris felt guilty for not being there, but he pushed through it. "Forget all that for now. Where is Todd?"

"He's right here talking to Billy and Carlos. Why?" Caleb asked curiously.

Paris looked at Daniel. Daniel took his hand and gave it a squeeze. "Don't freak out when I say this, but we think it was Todd that killed Michael and burned down the venue."

"What?!" Caleb shouted through the phone.

Paris steadied his nerves. "We think he was fucking one or both of the Michaels, and they broke up with him."

"He did say he just got out of a relationship the day before," Caleb said suspiciously. "What else do you have?"

Paris grimaced. "He has a reputation for being obsessive, and several of his exes have restraining orders against him. Nothing more than that."

"I'll contact my friends on the force and see if it pans out. Thanks." Caleb paused. "When can we expect you over here?"

Paris looked at Daniel. "I'm not coming over without Daniel."

"I understand." Paris heard the regret in Caleb's voice. "For all it's worth, kid, I'm here for you. Anything you need. I'll call you when I hear back about our mutual friend."

Paris sat his phone down. "He's going to call back when he finds something out."

"Do you want to head over there?" Daniel asked cautiously.

Paris took his glasses off and sat them beside his phone. "In a little bit. There's something I want to know first."

198

"What?" Daniel asked.

Paris moved to straddle Daniel's lap. "Who are the Service Boys?"

"My roommates." Daniel grinned. "Terry and Andy were the two in the video, and David filmed us."

Paris smacked Daniel's chest. "I knew I recognized Terry from somewhere!"

"That video was just for the audition," Daniel explained. "I don't normally fuck my roommates."

"Good." Paris smiled, then frowned. "Wait. Normally?"

Daniel twisted them so he lay on top of Paris. "Not anymore, and no one else." He kissed Paris. "Daddy Twink is retiring, so he can be your service boy."

"Oh, Daddy," Paris purred, brushing Daniel's hair back.

SO, NOT DANIEL

MARK SAT AT the kitchen table with his head down buried in his arms, wailing. "I can't believe it's over!"

"Dennis and Benjamin are trying to talk to Hunter," Lexi said, rubbing Mark's back. "It'll be okay."

Todd shuffled about. "Daniel is Daddy Twink? Is that right?"

"Do you need to be here?" Lexi asked Todd, shooting daggers at him.

Todd shrugged. "I guess not."

"Then please leave," Lexi hissed. "I don't like you and want you gone."

Todd snorted. "Fine. Fuck you very much, too."

"Okay, now that the annoying nasty muscle boy is gone," Lexi said soothingly. "Stop crying. We're going to figure everything out."

Mark continued crying into his arms. "I fired Paris! What was I thinking?!"

"You weren't." Lexi lifted Mark's head up. Tears streamed down his face. "Mark, know this comes from a place of love." She slapped him. "Get your shit together!"

Stunned, Mark stared at her. Before he could say anything, Ryan appeared in the doorway, "Um, guys, you should come in here. The police are here, and they're arresting Caleb's annoying boy toy."

"What?" Mark shot up with Lexi behind him. They entered the living room, where two officers had Todd in handcuffs on the ground. Caleb stood a few steps away, shaking his head disappointedly. "What's going on?"

Caleb looked at Mark. "Paris called me and told me about some suspicions he and Daniel had." Caleb shook his head. "Turns out Todd here was sleeping with both Michaels. They have security footage of him going into," Caleb paused, trying not to laugh, "Rainbow Unicorn Kitty Hall right before the fire started."

"So it wasn't Daniel," Lexi clarified.

Caleb shook his head. "No, and I'm pretty sure he's involved with Michael's murder, too."

"I'm not talking! I want my lawyer!" Todd screeched. "I know my rights!"

"So not Daniel either, then?" Lexi bumped Mark's shoulder.

With remorse, Mark said, "I owe him a major apology. Paris, too."

"You won't get rid of me this easily!" Todd screamed.

One of the officers lifted Todd to his feet. "You know you do have the right to remain silent." They pushed Todd forward. "Use it."

"Caleb, what did you ever see in him?" Ryan asked. "Besides your dick?"

Caleb shrugged. "He was pretty, and he didn't talk much with my dick in his mouth."

"A man after my own heart," Ryan said, fluttering his eyes at Caleb.

Mark wiped at his eyes. "I need to call Paris."

"He's not answering his phone." Lexi put a comforting hand on Mark's back. "We've all been calling and texting him since he left. He hasn't responded."

Caleb cleared his throat. "He called me, remember? He'll answer my call."

"See if he'll come over." Mark smiled weakly. "With Daniel."

36

PARIS TO THE RESCUE

"**P**ARIS!" BILLY SHOUTED, tackling Paris in a hug as soon as he walked through the door.

A moment later, Carlos did the same to Daniel. "Daddy Twink!"

"My name is Daniel," Daniel wheezed out. "Could you put me down, please?"

Paris wiggled in Billy's bear hug. "Billy, not that it's not great to see you, but I really should see Mark and Hunter."

"Mark's in the living room waiting for you," Billy said, letting go of Paris. "Hunter's still locked in his room. He won't even let Dennis in."

Paris grabbed Daniel's hand. "We'll go talk to Mark first. Then, I'll smooth things over with Hunter."

"What should we do?" Carlos asked.

Paris ordered, "Get everyone in the kitchen. Once I fix Hunter's and Mark's relationship, we've got a wedding to save."

"Sir, yes, sir," Billy and Carlos said, snapping to attention and saluting Paris.

Paris groaned, "When do your boyfriends get here?"

"Tuesday," Billy said impishly.

Carlos patted Paris on the back. "Welcome to the family."

Paris pulled a reluctant Daniel into the living room with him. When Lexi saw them, she patted a disheartened Mark on the back, then stood. Mark looked up at Paris with his tear-stained face. Mark stood and hugged Lexi, who then left without saying a word. Mark pulled Paris into a hug.

"I'm so sorry," Mark cried. "I shouldn't have yelled at you."

Paris hugged Mark back. "I forgive you. You were upset."

"That's still not a good excuse." Mark let go of Paris. Addressing Daniel, he said, "I owe you a major apology. You've been nothing but sweet to all of us, and I let my paranoia get the better of me. I'm so sorry." Mark extended a hand. "Forgive me?"

Daniel took his hand. "Of course. Whoa!" Daniel yelled when he was pulled into a hug.

"We're huggers in this family." Mark laughed, squeezing Daniel tight.

"Mark, please, don't break my boyfriend," Paris teased.

When Mark let him go, Daniel asked, "So I'm your boyfriend now?"

"I licked your ass." Paris smirked. "That means it's mine, Daddy." Mark covered his smile with his

hand. Daniel gaped at him. "What? You're the one who announced that you bottomed for me to everyone, not that long ago in this very room."

Daniel nodded. "Fair."

"Mark, come with me." Paris took his hand. "Daniel, we'll be back in a minute."

Letting himself be pulled along, Mark said, "He's locked himself in the bedroom. He won't even open the door for Dennis."

"He'll answer me," Paris said, stopping at the door. "Or else." He tried the knob but found it locked. He pounded on the door. "Hunter! Open the door, or I'm coming in!" They waited a moment. When no answer came, Paris said, "Wait here."

Paris went into the closet bedroom and grabbed a cotton swab from the bathroom. Pulling off the cotton from one end, he returned to the bedroom door. He dropped to one knee. He pushed the bald end of the cotton swab through the small hole in the middle of the knob. He found the lock release. Pushing it in, he twisted the knob and opened the door.

"How did you do that?" Mark asked, amazed.

Paris stood up. "They're old door knobs, like the one my uncle has in his house in Maine. When we visited, I had to share a room with my cousin, and he'd lock me out of the room, and I'd have to break in. I think my cousin turned it into a bed-and-breakfast with his boyfriend." Paris pushed the door open. "Hunter, are you in here?"

"Go away!" Hunter shouted from under the covers of his bed.

Paris walked over and pulled the covers off Hunter. "Get your ass out of bed," he barked. "We have a wedding to save."

"There's not going to be any wedding," Hunter grumbled.

Mark sat on the bed and rubbed his lover's back. "Baby, Daniel and Paris have forgiven me. Why won't you?"

"Because you still think Daddy Twink is out to get you," Hunter spat out.

Mark winced at the angry retort. "I don't think that anymore. It was Todd all along, and he wasn't out to get us. He was after the Michaels."

"Great. Now you're blaming him. Why? Because he almost hit you with his car?" Hunter asked angrily.

"No, because the police dragged him out of here in handcuffs about thirty minutes ago," Mark explained.

Hunter rolled over. "What?!"

"It's all very complicated. We just got caught in the crossfire." Mark gave him puppy dog eyes. "Forgive me?"

Hunter sat up and hugged him. "I guess; I mean, I do love you."

"I love you, too, Hunter." Hesitantly, Mark asked, "Does this mean the wedding is still on?"

Before Hunter could answer, Paris said, "Hell yes, it does. Now, get your super-sized gay asses in the living room. I have a wedding to save."

"Damn, he got a little ass and now he thinks he's a daddy." Hunter laughed.

Paris puffed out his chest. "I'm no daddy. Daddy is my bitch."

In the living room, Paris felt all the eyes of the gathered people on him. He tapped his tablet screen and brought up the list of the things that needed to be done and the names beside them. He looked up from the screen to the eagerly awaiting faces. Daniel gave him a nod. Paris straightened, then addressed everyone.

"Okay, everyone. Listen up. I've got a list of things we have to get done in the next seventy-two hours, so no screwing around." He fixed his gaze on Billy and Carlos.

Billy said defensively, "I feel attacked."

"Shut up." Carlos bumped him. "We'll stay on task. Promise."

Paris nodded. "Good. Now I'm going with everyone's strengths here. Lexi and Ryan, you're in charge of decorations. We need flowers, lights and anything else you can think of that we'll need. I'm sending a list of places to your phones now." Paris tapped at the screen. "Daniel is in charge of food."

"My roommates are going to help me prep and serve, as are a few of the other go-go boys from Fae Boys. The bartenders also said they'd help by tending the bar," Daniel added.

Paris nodded. "We've got Bonita Flores and the DJ from Fae Boys providing entertainment." Paris looked at Brad and Cody. "Luckily, the baker and photographer weren't caught up in this mess, but I need you two to build us a dance floor and a wedding arch." He turned to Caleb. "Caleb, can you help them?"

"Absolutely." Caleb smiled.

Hunter jumped in. "Wait. We don't have a venue for the wedding, or do we?"

Paris smirked. "We do. Right here. You know what they say, there's no place like home."

"What about us?" Billy asked. "What are we going to do?

Paris tapped on the screen. "You two have the most important jobs of all." Paris grinned. "You two are going to call all the wedding guests and tell them about the change in venue, and when you're done, I've got a list of errands I need you two to run."

"Okay," Carlos said.

Paris turned his attention to Dennis and Benjamin. "I need you two to find us chairs, tables, table clothes, dishes, and glasses. Here are a few places that might be able to help." Paris sent the information to their phones.

"We're on it," Benjamin and Dennis said together.

Paris looked at his screen. "I think that's everything; oh wait. There's one more thing. The most important thing. For Hunter."

"Name it," Hunter said eagerly.

Paris's smile stretched ear from ear. "Go take your fiancé to the bedroom and fuck his brains out."

"Gladly." Hunter pulled Mark into his arms.

Paris tapped away on his screen again. "After that, I just sent you a list of things you need to get done before the wedding. Massages, facials, haircuts, and picking up the tuxes you two keep forgetting to pick up." Paris looked at Mark and Hunter sternly. "You will not get married naked. Understood?"

"Yes, sir." Mark winced. "I knew we forgot something today."

Paris looked at everyone sitting there. "What are we waiting for, people? We have someone to marry! Let's get going! Move! Move! Move!"

Everyone fell over themselves to get to their appointed tasks. Daniel came up and took Paris by the hips. "You're so sexy when you're bossy."

"You need to get your ass to that kitchen and start making food for everyone." Paris gave him a quick peck. "They are going to be hungry."

Lexi tapped Paris on his shoulder. "Sorry to interrupt, but I must say, after seeing that, I'm going to love working with you."

"Thanks, it's just what I do." Paris blushed.

She fluttered her hand. "Well, keep it up, and I expect you two to have a real cooking pilot done after the wedding." She winked at Daniel. "By the way, I saw the Daddy Twink video. Very impressive. Let me know if you ever want to film something a bit spicier."

"Sadly, Daddy Twink has retired." Daniel shrugged.

Paris pulled Daniel closer. "He will be doing special appearances in my bedroom."

"Spicy," Lexi commented. "Just a word of advice. Don't let those special appearances occur just in the bedroom."

EPILOGUE

HAPPILY EVER AFTER

MARK LET HUNTER twirl him around the dance floor while their friends and family watched. "I love you, Hunter Adams," he said, smiling into his husband's eyes.

"I love you, too, Mark Adams." Hunter beamed back. "Wait, are you taking my name, or am I taking yours?"

Mark let out a laugh. "Hunter Greene? Yeah, that'll go over well."

"True." Hunter nodded over to where Alex was standing, away from everyone with Jordan, Cameron, Lexi, and the young man he brought. "I'm happy Alex came. Too bad the boys aren't happy he's here." They spun to see Dennis, Benjamin, Billy, and Carlos glaring daggers over at Alex. "Maybe we should have Paris fix it?"

Mark spun them to look at Paris, sneaking a kiss with Daniel. "He's a little busy."

"He deserves a vacation and a raise," Hunter commented. "He did a wonderful job putting all this together."

"True." Mark spun them around again. "Do we need to worry about those two?"

Hunter laughed. "Ryan and Caleb? They're big boys."

"True." Mark stared into Hunter's eyes. "I could dance with you all night."

Hunter dipped Mark. "Then we won't get to the honeymoon."

"In that case, can we dip out early?" Mark asked, grinning.

Hunter twirled Mark. "No. Lexi said she wanted to see us all for a special toast."

"Right. Well, it must be soon." Mark nodded over to the bar. "Cody and Brad have drink trays."

Hunter kissed him. "One more time around the dance floor?"

Paris joined Cameron and Jordan when they crossed the backyard to join the boys. "I'm so glad you two are finally here. Your boyfriends are terrors," he commented causally.

"Tell me about it," Cameron chuckled. "My Latin Lover does make me laugh, though."

Jordan smiled. "I heard your attack twunk put them in their place. Did he really chase them out of the kitchen with a butcher's knife?"

"Spatula." Paris laughed.

Jordan found himself wrapped in Billy's arms. "Teddy Bear!" He spun Jordan around before sitting him down on the floor. "Did Paris tell you about topping his big dick twunk boyfriend? You got to see his dick. It's massive! It's bigger than Carlos's!" Jordan grabbed Billy's face and kissed him.

"Is that how you get him to shut up?" Paris asked, laughing.

Carlos took Cameron's hand. "Hey, Chipmunk." His voice was soft and apologetic. "I missed you."

"You could have come over and talked to me," Cameron said, angrier than he intended to. "Look, I know you think something's going on between me and him, but that's been long over between us. He was going through some stuff and needed my help. I'm with you, Latin Lover."

Carlos kissed Cameron softly. "I know. I'm just being jealous."

"Anyway, boys, we're all needed in the living room for a special toast, then Lexi wants us to tell you what Cameron and I were up to," Jordan announced.

"Wait! You can tell us what you two were doing now?" Billy jumped up and down excitedly. "Tell me! Tell me! Tell me!"

Jordan kissed Billy again. "Calm down, or I'll get Daniel's spatula."

"It was a butcher's knife," Billy sulked.

Jordan patted Billy's cheek. "Sure it was, Pookie. Now go get Ryan and Caleb and meet us in the living room."

"Paris, will you grab Daniel?" Cameron asked. "Lexi said she wants the whole family there."

Everyone gathered in the living room. Lexi raised her champagne flute. "To the happy couple. It's about damn time."

Everyone raised their glasses and chorused, "It's about damn time."

After taking a drink from their glasses, Lexi continued, "Now, I'd like to give the floor to Cameron and Alex." She looked at Carlos pointedly. "I know some of you have been wondering what has been going on with these two, so I'll leave it to them."

Cameron and Alex moved to the center. Cameron nudged Alex, whose voice broke when he first spoke. "I know I'm probably the last person any of you want to see here." He held up a hand to stop Hunter from interrupting. "I was an asshole and a jerk to many of you."

Alex reached out a hand. The young man he brought with him came and joined him. "After I got hit by that car, I went back home and did some soul searching. This man beside me made me look in the mirror, and I didn't like what I saw." He squeezed the man's hand.

"Lexi, Cameron, and Jordan have already accepted my apologies. I hope you all can, too." Alex looked at Dennis. "I never meant to hurt you, Dennis." He looked over at Billy and Carlos. "Billy, I've been a horrible friend to you. Carlos, I know the secret conversations Cameron and I have put a strain on your relationship, but trust me. It was all plutonic." He brought the young man's hand up to his lips and kissed it. "I'm with Owen now."

Cameron cleared his throat. "Owen is the newest member of our team. He and Alex documented their journey. We're going to put it out there as one of our first shows." Cameron smirked. "Oh, imagine my surprise when I found out Owen is Alex's uncle. Jordan! I believe you're next!"

Jordan pulled Billy up to the center with him as everyone pelted Cameron, Alex, and Owen with questions they weren't answering yet. "Guys!" Jordan shouted over the chatter. "Focus! Or I'll have Daniel take a spatula to you all!"

When the laughter died, Jordan took Billy's hands in his. "Billy, after I wrote that article about you and the Country Boyz killings, there's been a lot of speculation about what happened to Shadow."

"Yeah, you said you couldn't find him," Billy said, confused. "He simply vanished. No one can find him. We gave up months ago."

Jordan swallowed hard. "That's because he didn't want to be found. He still doesn't."

"I don't understand what you're saying." Billy shook his head.

Jordan looked at Lexi, then back at Billy. "I know what happened to Shadow. He contacted me, and while you were here, I was video-interviewing him. He wanted to share his story in hopes people will finally stop looking for him."

"Where is he?" Billy asked frantically. "Where is he?"

Jordan shook his head. "He's living a quiet life now. With his husband. He told me to tell you that he loves you, and when he's ready, he'll reach out to you."

"You got to tell me," Billy pleaded, tears trickling down his cheeks

Jordan squeezed his hands. "I wish I could." Jordan pulled Billy into a hug. "I wish I could."

"Who is Shadow?" Paris whispered to Daniel.

Daniel shook his head. "I don't know. Search the web."

"He said, 'Shadow and Country Boyz, right?'" Paris asked, taking out his phone. "That's with a Z, right?"

Daniel shrugged. "I guess."

"Oh, shit." Paris covered his mouth.

Daniel looked over at the screen. "What?"

"That's my cousin," Paris answered. He looked at Daniel. "Want to go to a bed-and-breakfast with me?"

BOOK CLUBS

1. Which do you think it was, Mark's paranoia or cold feet, that kept him focused on Daddy Twink ruining their wedding? Why?

2. Paris was obviously attracted to Daniel. Do you think he held back because he was scared he'd lose a friend or scared to act? Why?

3. Daniel was obviously attracted to Paris. He is confident, but Paris made him nervous. Why do you think that was?

4. We learn that Carlos was fighting with Cameron because Cameron was talking with his ex. Cameron told him it was strictly plutonic and private. Would you trust your significant other to do that even if they told you it was plutonic and private?

5. When Daniel is around, Paris seems to be more confident around other people. Why do you think that is?

6. Dennis tells Paris he is going to start filming again, and that Benjamin is okay with it now that he knows all the work that goes into making an adult film. Could you honestly date or marry an adult film star and not get jealous?

7. Hunter and Mark talk about how Paris and Daniel are similar to them. Do you agree? Why?

8. Why do you think everyone but Paris sees that Daniel likes him?

9. Jordan has to tell Billy that he knows what happened to Shadow, but he can't tell him where Shadow is or how to contact him. Could you do that to your significant other?

10. Alex offers an apology to everyone at the end. Would you be able to accept his apology knowing what he did to Dennis? To Billy and Jordan? To Cameron?

BIO

ROBBY LEWIS IS a writer based out of Charleston, South Carolina. When he's not busy with his plants, being a doggy daddy, or watching the latest Sci-Fi, he can be found creating gay erotica for his readers that challenge the conventional sexual roles. He's been influenced by such writers as T.J. Klune, Rhys Ford, Jordan Castillo Price, and L.A. Witt. You can keep up with Robby Lewis's latest releases and antics on his social media at <u>Dreams – Robert J. Lewis (robert-j-lewis.com)</u>

More books from
4 Horsemen Publications

Erotica

Ali Whippe
Office Hours
Tutoring Center
Athletics
Extra Credit
Financial Aid
Bound for Release
Fetish Circuit
Now You See Me
Sexual Playground
Swingers
Discovered
XTC College Series Collection

Aria Skylar
Twisted Eros
Seducing Dionysus

Chastity Veldt
Molly in Milwaukee
Irene in Indianapolis
Lydia in Louisville
Natasha in Nashville
Alyssa in Atlanta
Betty in Birmingham
Carrie on Campus
Jackie in Jacksonville
A Humorous Erotica Collection

Dalia Lance
My Home on Whore Island
Slumming It on Slut Street
Training of the Tramp

The Imperfect Perfection
Spring Break
72% Match
It Was Meant To Be... Or Whatever

Honey Cummings
Sleeping with Sasquatch
Cuddling with Chupacabra
Naked with New Jersey Devil
Laying with the Lady in Blue
Wanton Woman in White
Beating it with Bloody Mary
The Erotic Cryptid Collection
Beau and Professor Bestialora
The Goat's Gruff
Goldie and Her Three Beards
Pied Piper's Pipe
Princess Pea's Bed
Pinocchio and the Blow Up Doll
Jack's Beanstalk
Pulling Rapunzel's Hair
The Urban Erotica Fairy Tale
Collection
Curses & Crushes
Queen's Incubus

Nick Savage
The Fairlane Incidents
The Fortunate Finn Fairlane
The Fragile Finn Fairlane
The Complete Package

DISCOVER MORE AT
4HORSEMENPUBLICATIONS.COM

Milton Keynes UK
Ingram Content Group UK Ltd.
UKHW011035201123
432908UK00005BA/746